MONEY
TROUBLE

MONEY TROUBLE

A NEBRASKA MYSTERY

William J. Reynolds

G. P. PUTNAM'S SONS   NEW YORK

G. P. Putnam's Sons
Publishers Since 1838
200 Madison Avenue
New York, NY 10016

Library of Congress Cataloging-in-Publication Data

Reynolds, William J.
Money trouble: a Nebraska mystery / William J. Reynolds.
p. cm.
ISBN 0–399–13353–4
I. Title.
PS3568.E93M55   1988   87–26958 CIP
813′.54—dc 19

Printed in the United States of America
1   2   3   4   5   6   7   8   9   10

As always, for Peg.

CHAPTER

ONE

It was a summer of thunderstorms and bank robberies. The thunderstorms were spectacular affairs—jagged bolts of lightning that rent the dusty, yellow-gray midwestern skies. The holdups were unspectacular—a lone gunman who dropped into various Omaha suburban banks and strolled out with the "undisclosed sum" you hear so much about in these cases.

The police had little to work with. Eyewitness descriptions were, as usual, fuzzy. The banks' surveillance-camera pictures were, as always, even fuzzier. The witnesses at least agreed that the robber was a slender white man in a dark-blue or black ski mask. That was good to know: From the pictures you couldn't even tell if the robber was human.

They couldn't agree about whether he drove off in a blue sedan, a black coupe, or a one-horse open sleigh. They couldn't agree about whether he had accomplices waiting in a getaway car—they couldn't agree about make or model, either—or whether he worked alone. They couldn't agree about whether he'd been gruff, polite, or as silent as a Trappist.

They could agree, and did, that the thief had carried a

big black handgun. Probably a .38 or a .45, based on the sketchy descriptions. And that was at the heart of the identification problem. When you're staring down what they used to call the business end of a gun, other details get trivial real fast.

Whoever he was, he was making a life of crime look awfully attractive. I knew of at least one underemployed free-lance writer and sometimes private investigator who wasted a lot of hours that summer daydreaming about ill-gotten gain.

That would be me.

It seemed easy enough. No heavy lifting. No paperwork. No income tax. And I already owned a gun.

I owned the gun—a couple of them, in fact—because I still owned the papers that said the state of Nebraska didn't mind too much if I conducted investigations, civil and criminal, within its boundaries. Of course, there were any number of *individuals* who felt differently. I was one of them. I had been doing investigation work in one form or another all my life. First as a reporter, then as a soldier, then as a rent-a-cop in someone else's agency, then as co-owner of my own shop, then free lance. Investigation, all of it. Sticking my nose where it didn't belong. Sticking it into someone's life—someone who seldom wanted it stuck there—because someone else *wanted* me to stick it there, and that someone else was signing the checks.

Is this any way for a good midwestern boy to make a living?

I didn't think so either, and I had the bank balance to prove it. Somewhere along the line I turned back to the typewriter—where I started, almost twenty years ago—supplementing my meager income with short articles for magazines whose names would mean nothing to you. Somewhere further along the line I decided that writing, though no more financially stable than sleuthing, was at least a pleasanter pastime. When I could steal the time, I worked on a novel—a detective novel, of course. I would become the

Hammett of the Heartland, the Chandler of the Corn Belt, the Macdonald of the Midwest—you get the gist. My goal became to develop my fledgling literary career to the point that it could support me and simultaneously to phase out the detecting.

Looks good on paper, I know, but the reality was far less smooth than the plan might lead you to think. Since I hadn't had the guts to set fire to my P.I. permit, "the old job" hung constantly in the background. I couldn't forget that I had something to "fall back on," and I did, often. When the checking account was terminal, when the writing wasn't going the way I would have liked, when I was tired or insecure or just plain bored, I went back to the old job, for all the wrong reasons. And I hated myself a little more each time.

It was a good thing I was too poverty-stricken to afford slugs for those guns of mine.

I was in the middle of another bout of private-detectivitis. Ironically, it followed the publication of my novel. After The Book had been accepted by a notably devil-may-care publisher, I had plunged into The Next Book with fervor, or perhaps it was fever, the likes of which I'd never seen, much less experienced. I backslid a couple of times, taking on a case or two to keep the landlord happy, but, by and large, it looked like the sun had gone down on my detective days, and not a minute too soon for me.

Then disaster struck.

The Book was published.

And the words stopped.

Now I languished in some kind of postpartum depression—stupor, call it—and every day the dust grew thicker on my old Smith Corona. Meanwhile, my on-again, off-again marriage was off again, with my wife, Jennifer, off again, to Aruba or wherever else was "in" that season. My twelve-year-old Impala had spent most of the summer in the hospital. One of the magazines I regularly free-lanced for had just gone the way of the *Titanic*, meaning a severe shrinkage of my already pint-sized income. And I was back on the investigations treadmill, knocking out a couple of bread-and-butter assignments, which, though quickly finished, had kept me away from my typewriter, which made me depressed, which . . .

Well, you can see why, at the midpoint of the summer and my doldrums, knocking over a bank or two seemed almost a good idea. Break the monotony and pick up a few quick bucks, too. What could be better?

Then the stickup artist went and got himself killed by the cops, spoiling the fantasy but no doubt saving me from perdition.

I read all about it in the mighty *Omaha World-Herald*. The robber—they were still calling him "the suspect," but in such a way as to indicate that they thought the chances of him having been innocent were about as good as your chances of pogo-sticking to the moon—had been shot to death by Omaha police on a stretch of road south of the old stockyards. His name was Gregg Longo, he was thirty-nine, he was white, he was unemployed, he was married, and he had lived in Omaha all his life.

Gregg Longo. The name and uncommon spelling prodded a long-dormant synapse somewhere deep in my memory, but nothing bobbed to the surface. I'd lived in the Big O nearly all my life, too, and I'd met a lot of people and snooped around in the lives of a lot more people. No telling where I'd come across Gregg Longo, the name or the man.

Besides, I had to play Paul Drake.

As played by William Hopper, Perry Mason's pal, Paul Drake was probably as close as television has ever come to an accurate portrayal of a private investigator. Drake did what most private detectives do most of the time, namely, legwork for someone who's too busy to do it himself. Like Drake, most P.I.s derive ninety-nine and forty-four one-hundredths percent of their work from lawyers trying to make or break cases. Most of the remainder comes from insurance companies, but the big ones, the ones most inclined to do any investigatory work at all, have their own staff investigators.

Playing Mason to my Drake was Mike Kennerly, who is a good deal smaller and quieter than Raymond Burr. Kennerly has thrown me any number of nourishing bones over the years. Years, hell: that month alone. This particular bone had to do with a divorce case that he was obliquely involved in. Kennerly's client had had an affair with a married man. Now the man was in the process of getting de-married, and the wife in turn was suing Kennerly's client for alienation of affection. Alienation of affection is a Middle Ages kind of claim. Basically, you say, Here sat my husband, fat, dumb, and happy, until this witch came and put a spell on him—"wickedly, maliciously, and intentionally"—and wrecked our storybook marriage, boo-hoo.

Well, of course, the best and fastest way for Kennerly's client to beat the idiotic rap would have been for Loverboy, the soon-to-be ex-husband, to climb up on the stand and testify that there was no affection to be alienated. That would be the gentlemanly, the sportsmanlike way to handle the matter. Unfortunately, Loverboy was neither a sportsman nor a gentleman. He dropped his wicked, malicious, etc., girlfriend like a hot rock the moment the lawsuits started flying, no doubt on the advice of his divorce lawyer.

All was not black, however. Kennerly's client was certain that she had not been Loverboy's first extracurricular activity—for the very good reason that Loverboy had told her as much—and Kennerly was working to induce one or two of her predecessors to testify. That would weaken the case considerably. The case would collapse under its own weight if the soon-to-be ex-husband had already taken up with a new little cookie.

Enter our hero.

Not to put too fine a point on it, my job was to keep an

eye on Loverboy. And a numbingly boring job it was, too. Most P.I. work is. I'd spent the past week or so keeping Loverboy on a leash. Loverboy, whose given name was Jonathon Desotel, was the restaurant-and-bar manager of the Omaha Olympic Club, one of those places where the well-to-do get together to congratulate themselves for being well-to-do enough to have their own club where they don't have to associate with the not-so-well-to-do. The routine I'd been running went like this: Pick up Desotel at the Olympic at around noon, follow him to lunch, follow him back downtown, then drop by again at about five to escort him home, where I'd keep an eye on him for two or three hours. Next A.M., tail him downtown and begin the routine again.

So far Desotel hadn't worked in any nooners, and the only moonlight action he was getting was with HBO.

I'd wasted the better part of another evening sitting in my car in the parking lot of Loverboy's apartment complex, alternately keeping an eye on the guy's balcony and a paper-back edition of *The Big Sleep*, which I was pretending to read. You can tell what kind of a funk I was in by the fact that even Chandler couldn't grab my attention.

The mood stayed with me all the way back to Decatur Street, where I checked the mail to see who all I owed money to and listened to the messages on the machine to see which of my creditors was getting antsiest fastest.

But there was only one message, at the end of a string of hanger-uppers—you know, the people who won't talk to the machine but who will later complain that I'm hard to get hold of. The caller didn't identify herself. She didn't need to.

The message began, "Ivan . . ."

Ivan. A faint shiver gripped me when I played back the tape that sultry summer night. It had been a lot of summers since I'd heard that voice. It had been a lot of summers since anyone had called me Ivan. No one else had, before or since.

Correction: Someone, the same someone, had called and left a message nearly a month earlier. If "message" is the word for it: "Um, Ivan? This . . . this is Carolyn . . . I— No. Never mind."

That was all. I had replayed the tape until the halting, disjointed words were caught firmly in memory, but they said no more to me on the second or third or tenth run-through than they had on the first.

And, at the same time, they spoke volumes.

Carolyn.

A voice and a name from twenty years out of the past.

The guys who say time travel is impossible must never have loved and lost, because at the sound of that almost-forgotten but unforgettable voice, I was instantaneously flung back in time two decades. Failed jobs, a bad marriage, an aimless, sometimes pointless life—all of it melted away, evaporated, like a snowball on a griddle. The slightly paunchy body of a middle-aged would-be writer and would-like-not-to-be private investigator may have been standing at the cluttered counter of a tiny kitchenette in a badly furnished apartment in a not-swell part of Omaha, Nebraska—but an eighteen- or nineteen-year-old kid was a billion miles away and teetering on the brink of a life that held nothing but promise.

Promise and Carolyn.

For a day or so after receiving the nonmessage, I tried to find her. I could have if I had pursued it diligently. But after a few strikeouts, I decided that if she had wanted to be found, she could easily have left a number on the machine. And if she didn't want to be found . . . well, why, after all these years, did *I* want to find *her?*

But now, a month later, here was the voice again. This time the voice was tempered with a kind of resolve, an almost palpable determination. There was no hemming and hawing. There was no hanging up in the middle. There was a message.

"It's been a long, long time, Ivan," Carolyn said. "The question is, has it been too long or not long enough?"

I dragged a thumbnail down the side of the squat brown bottle between my hands, shredding the label. "Ivan," I said. "How did you ever get started calling me that?"

She smiled. It was a soft, sad, weary kind of smile. Carolyn had changed only a little since long ago. Her dark hair was shorter, wavy now, and not quite so dark. Her lush figure was now perhaps ten or twelve pounds *too* lush, and a small, intriguing double chin had settled under her own wide, square jaw. The laugh lines around her mouth and eyes were deeper and didn't quite disappear when her smile did. Other than that, for all outward appearances, she was the same Carolyn Greco, and I could have picked her out of a crowd of thousands.

"Don't you remember?" she said huskily. "High school. Someone said your first name sounded like something out of *The Brothers Karamazov*—"

"They did make us read that, didn't they?"

"—and 'Ivan' was born. It's better than what your parents stuck you with, and *tons* better than your last name. 'Nebraska.' For cryin' out loud, who names himself after a *state?*"

My grandfather, for one. When he was fifteen years old he came over from the old country—alone—determined to make it to California. He made it as far as Omaha, working on the railroad all the live-long day, and when he got here, he decided, in a bizarre and probably alcohol-fueled fit of patriotism, to name himself after his new home. Nebraska. Well, why not? People are named Ireland and England and London. Virginia, even, and Georgia. His original tag had consisted of nothing but consonants, so Nebraska is certainly no worse. And look at the bright side: What if he had ended up in South Dakota?

But Carolyn knew the story as well as I did. I didn't go

into it. Instead, I matched her light, easy tone and said,
"I don't know. Shall we ask Joe Montana? Or maybe Bob
Montana?"

She laughed. "Who's Bob Montana?"

"Used to draw the 'Archie' comic strip. I think he's dead
by now, so we'd better stick with Joe."

"I'll ask him next time I see him." She smiled at me.
"Don't you miss high school?"

I downed some beer. "Not a lot."

She finished her drink and signaled the bartender. The
bar was just a bar, a neighborhood joint in the shadow of
the Mutual of Omaha tower. Vat 69 on the rocks and Miche-
lob Classic Dark was about as exotic as the menu got. There
was the ubiquitous color TV over the bar, and the Musivend
in the corner featured a queer mix of top forty, moldy oldies
and such oddities as Julius La Rosa's "Eh, Cumpari!" I
had suggested it as a meeting place because it was dark
and private, underpopulated and cool, a slightly dank oasis
in a still, hot town. The mercury had crept steadily upward
all day, dragging with it that almost electric tension that
signifies another storm brewing.

"I do. High school was about the last time I really felt I
knew what I was doing, where I was going. I feel like I've
been blundering around ever since."

"You were then, too," I said. "We all were. We were
just too stupid or cocky to know it."

"You're probably right." Carolyn shook a cigarette out
of a pack of Kool filters on the plastic tabletop between
us. "At least *you're* doing what you always said you would."

I peeled a match out of a book, ignited it, and held it to
the tip of her cigarette. Who says chivalry is dead? "Where'd
you get an idea like that?" I said.

"You're writing. Got one book out, another in the pipe,
I call that pretty good. But you always said you were going
to be a writer."

"I was going to be a reporter. There's a difference." I
dropped the match into a black glass ashtray that said Olympia

Beer in white on the rim. "Truth is, I've been both, a journalist and a writer, and I'd rather be a writer. But I've sure taken a roundabout way of getting there, and I ain't there yet, not by a long shot. What about you? Last I heard, which was a long damn time ago, you were back east gearing up for law school. I didn't even know you'd moved back to Omaha."

She nodded. "About, oh, six years ago. Mom was real sick. I moved back to take care of her until the end."

"I'm sorry. Why didn't you call, let me know you were back?"

A one-shoulder shrug behind a veil of blue smoke. "I thought you probably hated me."

"Bring the lady another Scotch rocks," I told the waitress the bartender sent over. "I'll have another Mic Dark." The girl went away, and I said, "I did."

" 'Did,' " Carolyn said. "Past tense?"

I nodded. "For a while. But hate's a pretty powerful emotion, and it takes a lot of effort to keep it going. Sooner or later you get tired. Or you get sent to a laughing academy. With any luck, you get smarter as you get older, and you gain a little perspective. When you're a kid, you can see things from only your point of view. You get a little older, all of a sudden you can see where someone else is coming from. Or was."

Carolyn looked at me and I looked at her, and there were maybe ten-thousand things that could have been said about what had happened twenty years ago . . . about how a couple of teen-aged friends suddenly became more than friends . . . about how the summer passed in a gauzy blur of hot days and hot nights, and the whispers, real and imagined, of dreams, fears, hopes . . . about how one left and one stayed and, despite all the promises and letters and long, late phone calls, nothing was ever the same after that . . . about tears and accusations, recriminations, denials and hard words and, finally, silence.

All that could have been said, and more. Things that

had never been spoken back then, or in the years since. But somehow, in that instant, none of it needed to be said any longer.

And couldn't have been: The waitress brought our drinks and cleared away the moment with our empties.

"Anyhow," I said brilliantly. "Twenty years. You already know about me—journalism school, army intelligence, private investigations, and my current stint as the world's greatest unknown writer. What about you? You went to college . . ."

She stirred her drink and set aside the skinny cocktail straw. "I went, but I didn't stay long. I just sort of, I don't know, ran out of steam my sophomore year. The folks blamed it on drugs, but that wasn't it. Sure, I did a little pot, everyone did, and some speed—remember speed, Ivan? We thought that was about the absolute limit, speed." She sipped from the glass and shook her head. "Speed. Seems about as racy now as . . . M&Ms or something, compared to what kids are doing to themselves with smack and crack and God knows what other junk. And this." She raised her glass and inspected it under the dim yellow light from overhead. "God, but we were innocent."

"Not so very innocent," I said. "Remember LSD?"

Carolyn smiled. "I was scared to death of it. Never touched it. Never got into anything heavy, you know? Speed scared me, the way it made me feel, and pot made my eyes itch. The grass, the speed, they didn't have anything to do with anything. They were just a convenient excuse, you know, something to blame for the fact that the good little girl didn't stick to the blueprint, didn't graduate with honors, didn't attend Harvard law, didn't hook up with a blue-blood firm, and isn't too likely to end up on the U.S. Supreme Court anytime soon."

"What *did* happen?"

Carolyn set her drink down in front of her and circled it with her fingers, almost but not quite touching the dewy glass. "I lost interest, is all. Being a lawyer, that was someone else's dream, not mine. All I ever heard was, 'You'd be good at this' or, 'You should be that.' No one ever said, 'Hey, what do you want to do, kid?' "

"What *do* you want to do, kid?"

She giggled, and I realized she had a slight buzz on, and so did I.

"Good thing no one ever asked me: I still don't know." She picked up her cigarette. The end glowed red. "Lord, though, I wish I was making a lawyer's kind of money. Take all my bills and lay them end to end . . . and I don't have enough money to pay them."

"*That's* a familiar song. What happened after college?"

"This and that. I bummed around, mostly on the East Coast. I went out to San Francisco—you know, Haight-Ash-bury, all that crap—but drifted back east. I floated. Nothing jobs, nothing friends, nothing relationships. About ten years ago I realized I wasn't a kid anymore. Revelation, right? So I went back to school. I was working as a legal secretary when Mom got sick. Now I'm a paralegal. With Miller Moore?"

I knew the firm. "Sounds good," I said, transferring beer from bottle to glass and from glass to me. "You never married?"

Carolyn looked at me, her glass parked midway between the table and her mouth. "Ivan, I thought you knew . . . I'm—I was married to Gregg Longo."

CHAPTER
TWO

"It was like a bad dream," Carolyn said. "A nightmare." She drained a little Scotch from her glass, then fixed her dark eyes on nothing in particular. "The policemen at the door, telling me Gregg was dead. Then the questions. What did Gregg do during the day? Where did he go? How long had he been out of work? How much did I earn at the firm? How much did we owe? Then more questions from the government men. Then the reporters . . . I wouldn't see them, wouldn't talk to them, couldn't . . . but even the neighbors, even our friends and relatives . . . all those questions—all those looks . . ." Her eyes came back to mine. "A nightmare. Ivan . . . it isn't ending, the nightmare isn't ending, sometimes I think it'll never—"

She broke off and cupped her palms over her eyes.

"Three weeks," she said from behind her mask. "Three weeks ago Wednesday. They came and they told me that they had killed my husband. They came and they told me that my husband was a bank robber. A *bank* robber! It's so . . . so weird, so weird. A bank robber—it's like Bonnie and Clyde, or John Dillinger, or *something*. It's like someone telling you your husband was a horse thief, or a train robber—

your first impulse is to laugh." She took her hands away from her face. Her eyes were red, but her cheeks were dry. "Can you believe it? Gregg a bank robber?"

I didn't have the heart to tell her I couldn't for the life of me come up with a face or anything else to put with the name Gregg Longo.

"They say he stole seventy-eight thousand dollars this summer—seventy-eight *thousand* dollars in those bank hold-ups?—and they want *me* to tell them where it is!"

"Do you know?"

"Of course I don't know. I don't know because Gregg never had any seventy-eight thousand dollars. When they killed him, he didn't have seventy-eight *cents* on him." She grabbed at her cigarette, snatching it out of the Olympia ashtray, and sucked on it nervously, angrily. "No, that's not true. He had a fifty and a few ones." She tapped gray powder from the end of the cigarette. It sailed dead center into its black target like a mortar shell. "The fifty came from one of the robberies. They traced the serial number or something." She released a lungful of smoke.

I said, "Fifty seems like a lot of cash to be carrying. If a guy's supposed to be hard up, I mean."

"That's what the cops said, too. I told them, he could've won it shooting pool. He could've gotten it anywhere, he didn't have to have stolen it. That's my whole point. That fifty could've come from *anywhere* . . . couldn't it?"

"Cash does have a habit of getting around," I said noncommittally.

"Well, if you don't want to believe it, feel free; no one else does." There was an inch left on the coffin nail, but she smashed it out in the ashtray. "Not the police. They've searched the house twice already. They searched my sister's house. They questioned all my neighbors, my friends, the people I work with. They've gone through bank records, tax records, credit records . . . they've got documentation on every stinking pack of gum we bought in the past six months. I think they've tapped my phone; there's a funny buzz on it sometimes. I think they've followed me a couple of times. I think they've rented the house across the street so they can keep an eye on me." She fumbled with the cigarette pack, her eyes locked on mine. "Ivan, I don't know how much longer I can stand it. That's why I called you."

I ignited a match and held it out for her. Her hands were slender, long fingered, the nails slightly rounded and painted with clear polish. The hands shook as she fiddled with the cigarette and held it into the flame I extended.

As the dead match joined its brothers in the black ashtray, I remembered Gregg Longo.

The memory was twenty years old and set in the wide, long halls of Central High School. Longo was in our class, Carolyn's and mine. Longo was a sullen, skinny little pinched-face sort of guy. Weaselly, but unmenacing. In those days of Beatlemania and the Mersey Sound and shaggy mop-tops, Longo was one of the last of the greasers. A borderline hood, he was in trouble a lot—not because he was bad news but because he hung around with guys who *were* bad news. While some of our classmates were studying to be leg-breakers, loan sharks, and con artists, Gregg Longo was the guy you'd vote Most Likely to End Up Behind Bars for Swiping Hubcaps.

Now that I remembered who he was, I didn't have a lot of trouble picturing him as a bank robber. A *successful* bank robber, well, that was something else again. I had trouble wrapping my head around that one. That, and the fact that Carolyn had been married to him for the past five years.

She read my thoughts. "Gregg had changed a lot since you knew him, Ivan. He had built a very successful business, a maintenance company that took care of a lot of businesses, a lot of offices around town. He was very good to me when Mom died. He was no saint, he had a lot of problems— things had been real bad the last six or eight months, ever since the business failed—but he was all right, you know?"

The bartender, a sawed-off white-haired man with a crew-cut, was engaged in a mock argument with the waitress, who I suspected was a daughter or a niece or something. The TV over the bar was on, volume down, the jukebox was playing "Money for Nothing." It was the summer you heard that song every time you turned around. On TV, Hawkeye started to say something to Trapper John, but I couldn't lip-read it because I looked at Carolyn and said, "Why do I get the feeling that this was not The Greatest Love of All?"

She gave me a long, hard look from the other side of the cigarette in her mouth. Then she took it away from her lips and said, "What were you expecting, Antony and Cleopatra? From what I hear, you and Jen aren't exactly Héloïse and whatsisname."

"Abélard. And this isn't a contest. I have a crappy marriage, if that makes you feel any better. It's been a joke for years, and I have a feeling the punch line's coming up. I apologize for being a wise-ass. At least you guys stayed together."

"For what it's worth now." Her eyes, unfocused, fixed on the television screen. Trapper John was saying something to Hawkeye. I didn't know what. I didn't recognize the episode. But it was an old, old one, from the days when Hawkeye and Trapper John and the rest of them were actually funny. "I called you," Carolyn said. "About a month ago."

"I remember. You didn't leave much of a message. I tried to find you in the book, but of course I was looking under your old name. I called a couple of the old crowd, but . . ." I let it drift.

"I, um, I wanted to hire you. You used to be a private eye . . ."

"Still am. That is, I've kept the license that says so. I just don't go out of my way looking for that kind of work unless I have to. You can starve just as well on a free-lance writer's income."

I waited while she wrestled with whatever she had to wrestle with in order to work things out in her own head. Finally she said, "Well, hell, it sounds crappy now, now that Gregg is gone . . . but I was going to hire you to, um, follow him."

I reached across the plastic tabletop, across the cigarette scars and the indelible rings, and covered her right hand. "Carolyn. Was it Gregg?"

Carolyn shook her head and swallowed, hard. Her eyes were moist but, again, no tears. "Not that," she said. "Not the banks. Gregg couldn't . . ." She blinked rapidly several times, then made a halfhearted go at a laugh. "I mean, if he *did* rob them, *I* never saw a nickel of it." She sniffed, and rummaged through her purse for a Kleenex. "No, I, um, I had another reason for calling you. I wanted you to find out if Gregg was seeing another woman."

"Ah."

She sniffed again. "This is really hard, you know? I—" Her voice cracked. We both waited a minute or so while she fought for control. "Gregg was out of work. He *tried*, he'd been looking everywhere, but there just wasn't anything. I was putting in an awful lot of overtime, trying to make enough to cover all the bills. Gregg . . . well, you couldn't expect him to sit around all day. He'd be out looking for work, or just . . . just *out*, you know?"

I nodded. "What made you think he was seeing someone else?"

"I didn't say I thought he was. I *wondered* if he was. It's stupid, I guess. I mean, before, Gregg was at work all day, I was at work all day . . . either one of us could've been fooling around with someone and the other'd never know. But it never even occurred to me until Gregg was out of work." She took a drink, caught an ice cube, crushed it between her molars. "He was very distant. It was only getting worse. At first I figured he was just really down on himself, his situation. I told myself, 'He'll find something soon and everything will be okay.' But he didn't, and it wasn't. I wondered if it was me. Then I wondered if it was someone else."

"Did you ever ask him?"

She shook her head.

"Since Gregg died . . . has there been anything . . . ?"

She shook her head some more. "You mean pictures, letters, mysterious canceled checks?" She made another attempt at laughing. This one didn't work too well either. "No, nothing. I haven't even found a picture of an old girlfriend."

The song had long since ended and the bar was silent except for a dull undercurrent of conversation supplied by the few other customers. Eleven o'clock on a weeknight, even a summer night, wasn't the joint's rush hour. Places like that, you'll see more traffic along about seven or eight o'clock. Dinner's over, the dishes are done, and mom and dad pop 'round the corner for a cold one. Not too many years ago, mom and dad would've brought the kids along for a Roy Rogers, but the law's tightened up on that sort of thing these days.

We sat with our thoughts for a little while; then I said, "Well, there probably wasn't anything going on. It wouldn't matter either way now, would it? I mean, Gregg's gone . . ."

She finished her drink, her third, and flagged the passing waitress. I let myself be talked into another beer. What the hell.

"Yeah, Gregg's gone," Carolyn said. "Gregg's gone. And I'm here."

Heavy stuff. I said, "Look, Carolyn, I know how rough this has got to be, but you'll pull through okay. I think you're doing real fine already. Just give it time . . ."

She gave me the sort of look you ought to give someone who's mouthing the sort of mindless platitudes I was.

"Time," she said. "That's good. How shall I fill my time? Waiting for another surprise inspection by the police? Overhearing my coworkers talk about me when they think I can't hear? Watching my neighbors watch me whenever I go out back to hang up the wash . . . as if they expect me to come out with a shovel and dig up the seventy-eight thousand dollars they're *certain* I've got buried there." Her voice broke—this time under the weight of anger, not sorrow. She reached for the pack of cigarettes. It was empty. She crushed it into a ball and flung it against the wall of the booth. "Smoke too much anyway," she mumbled through her teeth.

Once again, the girl came with our drinks. When she had left, Carolyn said, "Christ, Ivan, I just want to be left alone. You know?" She sighed deeply. "My husband is dead, and I can't even grieve because no one will leave me alone to do it. Everyone's convinced Gregg was guilty. Well, maybe he was. He was out of work, and Lord knows I don't make much at the firm. Things were tight, *real* tight. Who knows? Like I said, Gregg was no boy scout. Lately he'd been hanging around with a couple of characters who looked like bad news to me. Maybe he thought his back was against the wall . . . maybe he thought he didn't have any choices . . . The thing is, *I* never saw any of the money, if there was any. I sure as shoot don't have it now. But no one believes that any more than they believe Gregg was innocent. So they're making my life hell. And they're going to go right on making my life hell until they either see that Gregg was innocent or they get back their goddamn seventy-eight thousand lousy dollars."

"And that's why you called me. This time, I mean, tonight. You want me to clear Gregg."

She sighed again and impatiently smeared a tear from one eye. "It sounds crummy, but I don't care about Gregg. People are gonna think what they want to think. If there's any good come out of the last two, three weeks, that's it—

I've learned how really petty people can be. Well, Gregg's past being hurt. He doesn't care what people think. And me, I'm just too *tired* to care."

"Then . . ."

"Then I guess what I'm saying is this: Either you clear him—" She raised her glass and held the rim against her lower lip. "—or you find out where he hid the money."

CHAPTER
THREE

We sat around the bar for about another hour and got about another hour's worth drunk. We talked. We talked about Carolyn and Gregg. We talked about Jen and me. We talked about Carolyn's life. We talked about my books, the one that had been loosed on an innocent world a few weeks earlier and the one that was, as I hedgingly put it before changing the subject, "in the works." We talked about people we'd known in school, the ones we'd kept up with and the ones we hadn't.

And we talked about the way Gregg Longo died.

"He pulled over and got out of the car." Carolyn dinked with her glass, making the cubes chase each other around the inside perimeter. "Just like they told him. The cops. Then—I don't know—it went wrong. They said Gregg got out, but then he reached back in and came out again holding something. In his hand, his right hand. The cops thought it might've been a gun—it was getting dark—and the bank guy was supposed to be armed and dangerous. So they shot him."

"Cops," I said. "How many cops?"

"Two."

"Omaha police don't ride tandem. That means one of them called for a backup. Why? Why did they stop Gregg in the first place?"

"Just like it said in the newspaper. There had been a holdup a couple days earlier and Gregg's car sort of matched a description the police had. Of the getaway car."

The girl returned with drinks. I couldn't tell you what round we were up to, but I was about ready to go down for the count.

Carolyn, for her part, showed no sign of flagging. She took a healthy slug of her new drink and said, "You want to know what he was holding?" I waited politely. "A wallet. One of those big zipper wallet things? Gregg had it on the seat next to him. He always took it out of his back pocket when he drove." She made some more of her drink go away. "He went back into the car for his driver's license, for chrissake, not a gun. Gregg never even *owned* a gun."

She seemed awfully positive for a woman who couldn't say for certain whether or not her husband had spent his summer vacation knocking over banks and sleeping with other women. But I didn't pursue it. For one thing, she was talking again, and it's rude to interrupt.

"He didn't have the money on him." She demolished another cigarette in the Olympia ashtray. "Not the seventy-eight thousand, I mean. And he didn't have it in the car. They didn't find any in the house, or the backyard, or the safe-deposit box, or my desk at work, or my sister's house. They didn't find *anything*, no money, nothing to show that there had *been* any money."

"Except that one fifty-dollar bill he was carrying when he died."

"That doesn't prove anything."

"No. And it's not likely Gregg would have left a deposit receipt lying around," I said. "Do the cops have anything else to connect him to the robberies, anything concrete? The gun the holdup man used? The ski mask? Identifiable clothing?"

She was shaking her head. "None of that stuff. And the guy just wore ordinary clothes, you know? Shirt and slacks. Only thing unusual was, he wore long-sleeved shirts, with the sleeves down and buttoned. In this weather! And gloves. Those cloth work gloves you can buy anyplace."

"Huh. Did Gregg have any tattoos?"

"No. Why?"

"The sleeves and the gloves might've been hiding tattoos, or other identifying marks, on the guy's arms or hands. Any scars or anything?"

"Gregg? No. Yes. A scar, a kind of puckered pit, on his right—no, left thigh. A kid stabbed him with a scissors when he was about eight years old—"

"Not too useful," I said. "Unless the gunman wore cutoffs. I assume they didn't find the gloves or any clothing that could be positively linked to the robberies. Okay. Then what sort of reasons do the cops have for pestering you?"

She was still playing with her glass, now making interlocking moisture rings on the table. The jukebox was silent, and the volume on the TV was up. The network was pumping out reruns of old television series and trying to get us to believe they were the late movie.

"That's easy," she said. "Desperation. They don't have anything else to go on. They keep the heat on me, that takes the heat off *them*."

"Uh-huh. I haven't heard about any holdups since Gregg died."

Her eyes came up and met mine. "Got killed. There haven't been any. The police, and a lot of other people, have been sure to let me know that. But it doesn't automatically make Gregg guilty, does it? I mean, what if the *real* crook decided he was pushing his luck staying around here, and moved on? Or what if he figures that everyone thinking Gregg robbed those banks puts him in the clear as long as he lays off? Seventy-eight thousand dollars is a lot of money, Ivan. I could get by for a long time on seventy-eight thousand."

"You and me both." I drank some beer. The beer, and the ones that had gone before it, were beginning to gang up on the back of my tongue. I figured I'd better start tapering off. "Yes, it could all be the way you say. Or it could be that Gregg *was* guilty, so naturally the holdups stopped when he got stopped."

"Then where's the money?"

I shrugged. "You yourself said you were at work all day, sometimes into the evening, and Gregg was out a lot. Plenty of time to knock off the banks and secrete the loot—plus the gun and the clothes he wore in the holdups—someplace nobody knows about. Not even you."

"Yeah. I thought of that . . ."

"What about accomplices? A couple of the tellers thought the gunman had someone or -ones waiting for him outside. The cops have any thoughts along those lines?"

Carolyn dragged her glass across the table, smearing the intertwined rings she had so carefully made. "They questioned some of Gregg's friends. The guys who used to work for him. The guys he's been hanging around with since he's been out of work . . ."

"Anything?"

"Nothing that's convinced them to take the pressure off of *me*."

I took a deep breath and exhaled it. The air in the bar was stale, stuffy. Cigarette smoke had dehydrated me, my throat, my eyes, even my skin.

"Let's get out of here," I said.

When the sun left, it didn't bother taking the heat with it. Heat oozed up from the streets and the sidewalks and hung in the midnight air. Sweat popped out on my face and under my arms and on my back as soon as we left the bar. Carolyn had parked in a lot a few blocks over. I walked with her. Cars, pedestrians, hookers, and kids on skateboards or squat, ugly BMX bikes all danced an elaborate minuet in the streets.

Residents sat on vinyl-upholstered kitchen chairs on their front stoops, fanning themselves with magazines. An old guy with a face like the face on an iodine bottle sat on the sidewalk across the street, head back, mouth open, eyes closed. He wore a shiny suit with wide lapels, no shirt, no socks, no laces in what was left of his shoes. One hand was wrapped limply around a paper bag from which protruded the neck of a long green bottle.

"Hot town," I said. "Summer in the city."

"I liked that song," Carolyn said.

"They wrote a song like that?" I said. She laughed, but the catalyst was liquor and not my inimitable wit.

We reached her car without incident. She fumbled with her purse, fumbled further for her keys, found them, and unlocked the car door.

"Well?" she said.

"Well," I said.

"Are you going to take my case?"

" 'Case,' is it? You watch too much TV. Listen, Carolyn, you want to waste money, waste it on a lawyer. If half of what you tell me is true, the cops don't have anything on Gregg and they certainly don't have anything on you. That makes their actions harassment. Get a lawyer and get the lawyer to get you an injunction. The cops stop bothering you, you get your head on straight again and life goes on. You said it yourself: What's the difference now if Gregg did it or not? You just want to be left alone."

Carolyn smiled dreamily and patted the side of my face. "You're cute," she said. "I work in a law office, and know what? The place is lousy with lawyers. They got me the big fat papers, but so what? All's it means is that the cops have to be more . . . What's the word I want . . ."

"Discreet? Furtive? Circumspect . . ."

"Sneakier."

"That was my next guess."

"The cops just have to be more sneakier, that's all. If I

think they're hassling me, *I* have to take *them* to court and prove it." She turned down the corners of her mouth. "Swell."

I swallowed some night air. It was moist, unrefreshing— not much better than the recycled, reconstituted, "conditioned" junk I'd been torturing my lungs with for the past three hours.

"What the hell," I said, getting rid of the air. "The week's already a write-off. Tell you what I'm gonna do. I'll poke around a little, just for a day or two. Ask some questions, talk to some friends of mine downtown—that's detective jargon—see what I can see. Maybe I can find something out. Maybe I can at least convince some cops I know that they're barking down the wrong trail."

"Thanks, Ivan. That's all I'm asking for."

Somehow she was in my arms.

The last time I had held her, the night had been much like this. Hot. Humid. Electric. It was the summer between our freshman and sophomore years in college. It had been a bad summer, uncomfortable, and I don't mean just the weather. Whatever we had had, love or infatuation or plain old sexual attraction, somehow it had derailed while we were apart during the school term. That is, it had derailed for Carolyn. Not me. I felt the same and Carolyn felt bad and I felt betrayed, and neither one of us had the maturity or the experience to understand and explain our feelings.

We had gone out on what I think I knew would be our last date. We saw a movie, we drove around, we parked. We talked about everything except the thing that was on our minds. We made love—funny expression for it—on the backseat of my uncle's '66 Catalina. Then I took her home and I held her, on the front steps of her folks' house on Center Street, under the pale yellow light they always left on when she was out.

"Good night," she said when it was time to say good night.

"Good-bye," I said.

"Good night," she said when it was time to say good night.

I took my arms from around her, she turned toward the car and dropped her keys.

"Son of a bitch," she said.

We got down on all fours and hunted for the keys. I found a piece of broken glass that glinted in the feeble light just the way you'd hope a set of keys would glint. In fact, the keys soaked up light like a black hole, and I found them only by brailling the filthy asphalt.

I stood. When Carolyn held out her hand for the keys, I closed my fist around them. "How 'bout I drive," I said.

"Sexist pig," she said mildly.

"I resent being called a pig," I said. "As for 'sexist,' well, you can open your own damn door."

I slid in behind the wheel and reached across to pop the lock on the passenger's side.

The house was a big old two-story frame number on Seventh near Hickory, a neighborhood that used to be called Little Italy. The fact is, it still was called Little Italy, but the term had grown increasingly less accurate as the blocks' ethnic complexion had changed. Call it what you will, it was a good, working-class neighborhood, and if the houses and the yards and the kids who played in the yards were a little shabby around the edges, it was because of a shortage of money, not concern.

I settled into the living room, a big square space at the front of the house, while Carolyn disappeared elsewhere. The place was decorated tastefully though not expensively. A handcrafted carpet left just a foot or so of hardwood floor exposed on all four sides. Pale, faintly pin-striped wallpaper gave the room a soft, inviting cast. The dark, wide woodwork either had been spared the painting frenzy that ruined a lot of doors and moldings in the forties and fifties, or someone had done a fine job of refinishing.

It was a good room. It was a lot like Carolyn—neat, attractive, without flash or gaudiness or pretense. I leaned back into the sofa, crossed my ankles on a three-legged footstool, and closed my burning eyes.

Eventually, Carolyn returned and sat beside me. "Water's on for coffee," she said. She had changed from the summer dress she'd worn at the bar and now wore blue terry-cloth shorts and a red Cornhuskers T-shirt.

We sat together on the sofa, the lights low, our eyes closed, and talked. Talk, talk, talk. Twenty years' worth. A lot of it was the same talk we'd had in the bar. A lot of it was about things—lives—refusing to turn out according to plan. A lot of it was about how things—lives—go wrong. Carolyn's life, my life, Gregg's life. The business went bad, the marriage went bad, the life—lives—went bad. He started drinking heavily, he started hanging around with unsavory companions, he stopped being Carolyn's husband and went back to being the weasel, the loser he'd been in school all those years ago.

On toward one, one-thirty, Carolyn began to come on to me. Just a little. I played back. Just a little. The night was sultry, and we'd both had a few drinks, or a few too many, and I'm human, or pretty close ever since I left Krypton. Her mouth was warm and inviting. So was the rest of her. The T-shirt came off easily and I caressed her. She had my shirt half-unbuttoned and was nipping gently at my chest, my belly . . .

And about the time things started to look interesting, her breathing became deep and regular, and I realized she'd dozed off.

This sort of thing never happens to Mike Hammer.

I held her for a while, then slowly disentangled from her and went in search of the coffee she had promised. It was that or a cold shower.

The coffee was instant, which is to say it was lousy. How

can the FTC let these guys get away with saying "Caffeino Instant tastes as good as fresh ground"? I've never had a cup of instant coffee that tasted as good as fresh *ground*, as in dirt, let alone fresh-ground coffee.

I downed two cups. They perked me right up, not that I needed much perking.

Figuring it gauche to leave one's hostess en dishabille on her living-room sofa, I hoisted her up and carted her to the front stairs. She mumbled and grumbled some as I hauled her into what appeared to be the master bedroom, but she neither protested nor assisted.

I eased her onto the bed, onto a light-blue pin-dotted spread. There was a small lamp on the bedside table, a ceramic lamp with a square blue shade. I turned it on, and she turned away from the light, murmuring in her sleep.

I took a long minute to study her. I took a long minute to remember other hot, still nights a long, long time ago.

On a mirrored dresser were some framed photographs. Carolyn's parents, now deceased. In the picture, they were much older than I remembered them. Some people I didn't recognize, perhaps Gregg Longo's people. A wedding photo, Carolyn and Gregg when everything was bright and shiny.

I studied Longo's face. It was familiar yet unfamiliar. I recognized him because I knew who he was, but if you'd stuck the picture in my face cold, I'd've never got it. Twenty years ago Gregg Longo had been a skinny greaser with bad skin. Fifteen years later—the wedding photo was five years old—he was slightly built, standing no taller than Carolyn, who may have been wearing high heels. But his dark hair was Vitalis-less, even if he did wear it in Lord Fauntleroy bangs, and his skin had cleared up nicely. He wore a gray tux and a pink bow tie with diamond tips, a pink silk square in the breast pocket of his coat, a pink rose at his lapel, and all I could think of was what a jerk-off he'd always been. Gregg Longo and Carolyn Greco. Married. Jesus.

Carolyn wore a long, intricately stitched ivory gown. No

hat or veil or headdress. Her hair had been darker and longer then. It contrasted sharply with the dress. All brides are beautiful, they say, but Carolyn more so than others, I thought. Somewhere inside me there was a twinge, a pang— a sudden, gnawing, vacant feeling.

I put down the photograph and turned toward the bed. Carolyn hadn't moved.

I finished undressing her. Then I lay down beside her.

Some time later, I got up, turned out all the lights, and let myself out of the house.

I got up the next morning, which was more of an accomplishment than those puny words indicate. I threw together a pot of coffee and stood under a hot shower for a few weeks and was sitting in my car slurping from a big thermal mug when Loverboy left his house at seven-thirty. I followed him downtown—by now I knew his route better than he did—made sure he got his little Toyota snugly parked, and watched from a no-parking zone as he entered the Olympic Club at eight-oh-three.

I wrote down every fascinating detail in my Official Detective Z-9 Notebook, finished my coffee, and pushed the car out into the driving lane.

You see the holes here as well as I do. I follow Jonathon Desotel to work, I follow him at noon, I follow him home and keep an eye on him for a few hours. I assume that when he goes to work he goes to work and *stays there*. What's to say he doesn't enter via the front door at eight-oh-three, exit via the back door at eight-oh-four, and slip off to do exactly what we hoped he was doing? What's to say he doesn't take a long coffee break mid-afternoon? What's to say he doesn't sneak out for a couple of hours after I leave in the evening, always returning home where I pick him up the next morning? Nothing. Except perhaps the law of probability. Desotel had no reason, no concrete reason, to suspect he was being watched. He hadn't made me; I was certain of that. Therefore there was no cause to suspect he'd take extraordinary measures in conducting his, er, affairs. If Loverboy was paranoid enough to believe without evidence that his every move was being watched, then he probably was paranoid enough to tread the straight and narrow, at least for the duration.

It was a gamble, but Kennerly and I thought it a reasonably safe one.

Besides, 'round-the-clock surveillance is an expensive undertaking, requiring at least three and preferably five pairs of eyes if you're going to make anything more than a half-assed job of it. Kennerly's client never could have afforded it. Random surveillance isn't as thorough, but it's loads cheaper. Especially at *my* rates.

There's always a dollar sign in front of the bottom line, isn't there?

I cruised around and down the block and crammed my heap in front of a meter across from OPD headquarters, which is not one of the city's sexier buildings. Somewhere in the back of my head was the invaluable though never-verified knowledge that Lovely Rita, Meter Maid, didn't hit the pavement until nine, so I ignored the parking meter's gaping maw and jaywalked over to the police station.

I went in and got a copy of the report on the shooting of Gregg Longo.

On TV the good guys have to resort to all sorts of conniving for a peek at police reports. In real life the reports are almost always available to the public, or any member of it who wants to pay the outrageous photocopying fee. If you're insomniac, I heartily recommend an armload.

Usually the details of a police shoot are far less cut-and-dried than survivors prefer to believe. The Longo shoot was no exception. Gregg Longo's Monte Carlo fit a superficial description given by a bank employee. An OPD uniform on routine patrol spotted it. He radioed for backup—the suspect was thought to be armed—and, when it arrived, signaled Longo to pull over.

Longo did. And, as Carolyn noted, he started out of the car, stopped, reached in for something, and came out holding it in his right hand. In the deceptive lighting, the cops couldn't see what it was, only that it was long and dark and appeared cylindrical. The cops ordered him to drop it. Longo did not. Cop A thought it looked like Longo was aiming at Cop B, hollered another warning and, when Longo turned and faced him, the object outstretched, pulled the trigger.

Longo was pronounced dead on the scene.

The Internal Affairs report had not been handed in yet. Cop A would probably be let off with a stern warning. It helped that Longo's innocence had not been determined.

I folded the pages into thirds and tucked them into my shirt pocket. Then I went looking for the cubicle that contained Detective Kim Banner.

Banner—I've tried calling her Kim and it doesn't work— was sitting behind a desk and a Styrofoam cup of coffee. I lowered myself into an uncomfortable green vinyl chair alongside the desk and crossed my legs.

"Well," Banner said. "The Big O's answer to Dashiell Hammett. What brings you out so early, Sherlock? Fighting crime, or just soaking up background?"

"You don't soak up the background in a place like this. It sort of sticks to you as you pass through."

Banner made a face. "Someone who didn't know better might think you didn't like our decor. How's the new book coming along?"

"So-so." I shrugged. "I haven't looked at it for a couple of weeks. I've been back in harness. Trying to make enough to tide me over."

"Until the royalties come pouring in. How far along are you?"

"Far enough." I grinned. "That's my new stock answer to The Inevitable Question. I've decided there's no real way to answer it. For one thing, I won't know how long the book is until I've finished it, so how can I tell you how far along I am? For another, if I sit down today and trash everything I wrote last week, I can go from half done to an eighth done in less time than it takes to tell."

"Sorry I asked." Banner sipped at her coffee, grimaced, and reached for a blue paper packet of sweetener. "It's better than usual this morning," she said, dumping the contents into her cup. "If you're private-eyeing again, is it safe to assume this isn't a social call?"

I hadn't known Kim Banner long—just long enough to know she was a good cop, in every sense. She knew her job and she did it well, with a kind of quiet, sure efficiency that you don't get by reading self-help books and attending assertiveness seminars. She was a small woman, compact, with sharp features and short, shaggy dark-blond hair. I'd met her on a case early in the year. When the case was over, we saw each other a couple of times, socially, I mean, but nothing heavy-duty had materialized.

"Not entirely," I admitted, and flung the Longo report onto her desk.

She unfolded it and skimmed it with quick, gray eyes. Then she folded it again and sailed it back at me across the desk. "Very nice."

"I'm looking into it."

"Why?"

"Because I've got a client who wants me to."

"No foolin'. Word is, Internal Affairs will turn in a report this week yet. Three-to-one for a clean shoot."

"I don't doubt that. I'm not interested in the shoot. I'm interested in the banks."

"Ah," Banner said. She lifted her cup and settled back in her desk chair. "Who's the client?"

"The wife." There are times to protect your client's identity and then there are times when it may do your client more good to be known. In this case, I saw no good reason to play coy about Carolyn's identity. And if the cops *were* hassling her, maybe they'd back off a little if they thought she was biting back.

"She thinks her husband got a raw deal on the news shows and she wants you to prove he was an innocent victim," Banner ventured.

"Something like that. Really all she wants is for you to leave her alone."

Banner's eyes widened. "Me? Hey, Ellery, you got the wrong chick. I'm Homicide, not Robbery."

I rolled my eyes. "Not you *personally*. Omaha Police Department."

"Oh, them. You probably won't buy it, considering the source, but I think your client has a persecution complex. Sure, she got run through the wringer pretty thoroughly there, but my understanding is she's in the clear as far as we're concerned. Feds too—and it's really the feds' ball game, you know, we just bat cleanup. I don't even think Longo's being actively investigated anymore, though of course everyone's keeping eyes skinned. But except for that fifty he had on him—" she nodded at the half-folded sheets on the edge of her desk "—there's been no sign of the money, nothing but the flimsiest descriptions to link him to the holdups, and his wife sure doesn't act like she's just come into an inheritance." She sipped some coffee. " 'Course, if she *thinks* she's under the microscope, maybe it's because she has a guilty conscience."

"Uh-huh. So guilty that she hires a private detective to turn suspicion, which you say there ain't any of, away from her. When was the last time you heard of that happening?"

"You mean in real life? Okay, look, you want me to say she doesn't have the money? She doesn't have the money. What's it to me? I'm just trying to do you a favor, and her. Nobody here suspects her of anything. She's paranoid."

"What about the feds?"

"Those guys are *definitely* paranoid. Whether they still

think your client might know more than she's telling, I couldn't say. What I can say is *we* don't think so."

"Not officially, at least. If Longo didn't rob those banks, you have any idea who did?"

"Male Caucasian, five-nine or five-ten, slender . . ."

"Well, that ought to narrow it right down for you." I stood.

"For *them*." Banner jerked a thumb over her shoulder, in the general direction of the Robbery unit. Then she swiveled her wrist so that the thumb was aimed at herself. "That's why I like Homicide," she said. "It's cleaner work."

FOUR

Lovely Rita had gone on duty early that day. I slipped the ticket out from under the wiper blade, gave it the once-over, stuck it under a wiper on the next car down and headed out.

The day was already hotter than an old maid's dream, as the old-timers still say, and the fitful southwestern breeze was nowhere near a match for the sun. The Impala had what we used to call four-sixty air-conditioning: you roll down all four windows and drive at sixty miles an hour. Still, I reasoned, it was better than the air-conditioning back at my place. It's not easy getting an apartment building to go sixty miles an hour.

Carolyn Longo had given me the names of her late husband's two unsavory companions. Marlon Abel and Al Patavena. I also had the names of a couple of bars where they and Longo habitually met for drinks, cards, maybe a couple racks of pool. I checked out both joints, but there had been no sign of either Abel or Patavena yet today. Sure, it was early. But from what Carolyn had indicated, time had little meaning for these jokers. At both bars I exchanged my name and card for promises to call if either of the men

turned up. I hadn't been out of the P.I. game long enough
or far enough to have forgotten what promises like those
are worth.

Outside the second bar I found a phone booth that actually
contained a phone book and looked up both men. Obvious,
yes, but sometimes the obvious is what does it. Not this
time, unfortunately. Neither was listed. I doubted that either
Abel or Patavena was the type who'd feel the need for an
unpublished number, so I assumed they either didn't have
phones or lived in places with communal phones.

So I was standing on the crumbling sidewalk outside the
phone booth, bracing myself for the hot vinyl seat in my
crate, when I noticed the Job Service office across the street.
With a mental shrug, I trudged across the softening asphalt,
ducked under a waterfall of condensation shed by a window
air conditioner over the front door, and entered the tiny
storefront office.

Twenty minutes later I was in my red bomber, enjoying
the breeze through the windows as I cruised past the gray
cylindrical grain elevators off of Interstate 480 just south of
town. A plump, balding, birdy-looking fellow at Job Service
had readily admitted that Patavena and Abel dropped in
whenever they were short on cash, seeking temporary jobs
for unskilled labor. "Temporary" was the operative word:
When the dynamic duo felt they had enough bread to tide
them over, they simply quit showing up for work.

As far as the employment-agency guy knew, both men
were still working a street-reconstruction job he'd sent them
to earlier in the week, on Hascall off of Seventy-fourth, in
the Westgate division.

I took the freeway, the Interstate, as we call it around
these parts, west around the south end of town. A viscid
haze hung over the lowland south of I-480. I nudged the
air-conditioning up to four–sixty-five.

The Seventy-second Street exit got me off of the Interstate; Grover Street, next to the Howard Johnson, got me

off of Seventy-second and threaded me along to Seventy-fourth, where I stashed the car in the shade of a willow. The street I wanted was lined by small, trim, thirty-year-old middle-class houses on one side and Saint Joan of Arc Catholic school on the other. Currently, the block was a shambles. The pavement had been ripped out curb to curb. In fact, the curb had been ripped out curb to curb, too. A dozen or so browned, sweating men were getting rid of the debris.

A shirtless black man with broad shoulders and a broadening belly proved to be the gang's foreman. He was grudgingly cooperative, which is to say that on the one hand he didn't want any trouble on his site but on the other hand didn't feel he owed anything to the guys I wanted. He pointed out a small knot of men taking a break farther down what used to be the street. "The skinny guy's Patavena and the short, square one's Abel," the foreman said. I thanked him and set off in that direction. The foreman stopped me with a heavy hand on my biceps. "You take them out of here, there's gonna be any trouble, right?"

"No trouble," I said.

The two stood with several other men near the gate of a GMC pickup parked in the alley behind the school. A large metal tank was perched on the edge of the gate. The men were pulling water from the tank, filling plastic cups, trying to beat the heat. Patavena was a tall, dark-haired, dark-skinned fellow with a narrow, pockmarked face. Abel was much shorter and stouter, with pale, dirty-looking brown hair and a miserly peppering of whiskers trying hard to be a mustache. I figured them both to be about my age.

Neither was especially eager to talk with me. I realized within seconds that I'd made an amateur's mistake: I should have interviewed them separately. Any schoolteacher knows or fast discovers that the class cutup is a hell of a lot less cocky when you pull him away from his audience. Together, Abel and Patavena were like a couple of high-school kids showing off for one another.

I said, "I want to talk to you two about Gregg Longo."

Patavena said, "Yeah? So talk."

Abel said, "We don't know any Longo, do we, Al?"

Patavena. Yeah, that's right. Too bad.

Abel. We gotta get back to work now, man. Nice talkin'
to you.

Patavena. Yeah. Let's do it again real soon.

Me (over guffaws). Your foreman doesn't mind your talking
to me.

Patavena. Yeah? Well, maybe *we* mind.

Me. Maybe you'd rather talk to the cops.

Patavena. (Nothing.)

Abel. (Nothing.)

I hauled out the wallet and showed them the little scrap
of paper that says I'm licensed to conduct private investigations and am entitled to all kinds of swell perquisites and
considerations not afforded to ordinary mortals. Actually,
that last part isn't in there, but it will be, come the revolution.
"I'm investigating Longo's death," I told them. "You know
that some people think Longo was the guy sticking up all
those banks earlier this summer. Some say the stickup man
had little helpers with him. Longo's wife says you and he
were pretty tight here the past few months . . ." I ended
it with a shrug.

"Hey, man, what'choo pullin' here? We already talked
to the cops," Abel squealed.

"Yeah, long time ago," Patavena said.

"We told them, we don't know *nothin'* about Gregg
Longo."

"Yeah, we don't know *nothin'*."

"I can believe it. But that's not what Longo's widow
seems to think."

"Hey, *fuck* her, man! I don't care *what* she says—"

"Yeah."

"We only knew Longo to have a beer with, you know?
Maybe shoot some pool. That's *it*, man!"

"Yeah," Patavena repeated.

"If he was knockin' over banks, he sure didn't tell *us* about it. And we sure as shit didn't see any of the *money*, man."

I pointed a finger at Patavena. "Don't say it," I said. "Just don't."

Abel said, "If Longo was pulling bank jobs, it's nothin' to do with us, okay? Go talk to his old lady."

Patavena said, "Yeah. Or go talk to his girlf—" He stopped because Abel elbowed him vigorously.

"Longo had a girlf?" I said. "Does the girlf have a name?"

"Hey, man, everybody got a name. But we don't know this chick's, right, Al? I mean, Longo just told us about some babe he was boffin' while his old lady was out working, you know? Hell, for all we know maybe it was more than one broad, right?"

"Right," said Patavena. It was better than Yeah, at least.

I said, "I assume you told the police about Longo's girlf back when they questioned you."

Abel crushed the translucent cup he'd been holding and threw the scrap to the ground. "Hey, cop, you ass-ume whatever you feel like, okay? 'Cause I'm tired of talkin' wit'cha." He slapped his friend's arm with a casual backhand. "C'mon, Al, let's get back to work."

"Yeah."

I stayed where I was, near the pickup, and watched them join the men who had already resumed work. Abel looked back at me a couple of times, then resolutely ignored me. He and Patavena exchanged words, but there wasn't necessarily anything to that.

On my way back up the block I stopped to speak with the foreman, thanking him for his cooperation, et cetera— the P.R. bit. Then I went around the corner and found the car where I'd left it. I got behind the wheel and pointed the machine toward my end of town.

I enjoy it in detective stories when the incorruptible, square-jawed protagonist sits in his car for hours, days, weeks on end, eating junk food and keeping an eye on his quarry. I don't know about other towns, but forty-five minutes is the upward limit for Omaha. At least, *I've* never been able to stake out a place for more than forty-five consecutive minutes before someone calls a cop who politely asks me what in hell I think I'm doing.

Over the years, I've come up with two ways around that potential embarrassment. One is the method I used while I stuck to Loverboy: I let the police know in advance where I'll be lurking. They give that information to the desk officers, who pass it along to the duty officers, who give it to the patrol officers, and there's usually no problem.

The other method is to think of ways to not have to waste much time sitting in parked cars.

I like the second approach better; I can think of lots of better ways to waste my time than sitting in parked cars watching other parked cars. And since I had to be downtown again to meet Loverboy before the bells of Saint Mary Magdalene signaled noon Mass, I didn't have time to hang around Westgate all day. So before I left Hascall Street, I asked the foreman what time the crew knocked off work and got there fifteen minutes before that hour. It meant letting Jonathon Desotel go home unescorted, but I had a feeling that Abel and Patavena might prove a little livelier than he'd been.

I would have been willing to bet real money that Abel and Patavena would be among the first to exit when the whistle blew, figuratively speaking. And I was right. They cut through the alley behind the Catholic church and school, came out on Vinton, the next block north of Hascall, and headed for Patavena's car, parked along the curb. I assume it was Patavena's, since he got behind the wheel. The car was an ancient Studebaker Lark, a low, square wagon that looked like nothing so much as a refrigerator on wheels.

The wagon was army green where it wasn't gnawed and scarred by the cancer of too many midwestern winters. On the rear door, STUDEBAKER was spelled out in inch-high chrome letters. Someone, Patavena or a previous owner, had pried off the first E: STUD BAKER. Guys used to do that back in high school, too. Even back then, I could never figure out exactly why.

I noticed the creative sign alteration when the Studebaker made the turn from Vinton onto Seventy-fourth, when I fell in right behind.

It was an easy tail. Which is about all you could say for it. They stopped at a liquor store, then they stopped at a decaying old two-story just off of Tenth Street, a big square rooming house that had Rooms To Let, according to the store-bought sign on the porch door. They went in. And that was it.

Me, I did a lot of detectivey things: I ascertained from the house's mailboxes that Marlon Abel lived there. I sat in the car until I felt sufficiently near heat stroke, then went into the Rexall across the street and pretended to browse through magazines, paperback books, and Hallmark cards. I sat on a bus-stop bench outside the Rexall and kept Patavena's Studebaker in view while I didn't read the copy of *USA Today* I'd bought when the pharmacist started getting edgy. What it boils down to is Abel and Patavena had planned a nice quiet evening with whatever they'd picked up at the package store. At least, they showed no indication of doing anything suspicious or sinister or of the remotest help or interest to me.

I played "ten more minutes" until seven-thirty. You know the game: I'm gonna wait just ten more minutes and see if anything happens. Nothing did, even after three ten-more-minuteses, so I got in the car and wheeled past Loverboy's place. His cute little Toyota was in the lot, where it always was. I tooled around the back of the building and took a gander at his apartment, three flights up. Desotel was sitting in a lawn chair on his little deck or balcony or whatever you want to call it, reading a newspaper.

I snorted in disgust. I was the only guy in town who wasn't sitting around with his feet up, enjoying the comforts of home sweet home. But I knew how to fix that.

I went home and shoved a sheet of cheap yellow paper into the typewriter and stared at it for ten, fifteen minutes while words failed to materialize on it. Then I got up and liberated a Falstaff from the fridge. I glanced at the front page of the paper. I read all the cartoons in last week's *New Yorker*. I picked up a yellow legal pad and, pretending to sketch out the scene in the book that I was having trouble with, sketched out a pretty good picture of the beer can on my kitchen table.

The doorbell rang and I answered it, which only goes to show how uninspired I felt. I'm very good at not hearing doorbells, phones, and other modern nuisances when the writing is going well. When it isn't, every little distraction is welcome.

I opened the door and looked at Koosje.

"Would you like to buy some Girl Scout cookies?" she said.

"I'll take your cookies any day, little girl," I said, and ushered her into the room.

She stepped in and removed her oversized dark glasses. Koosje—Koosje Van der Beek, *Doctor* Van der Beek, to the likes of you—is a psychologist. A very good psychologist, she tells me, and I believe her. She has the respect of her colleagues and the admiration of her clients. She has a reputation for compassion, intelligence, dedication, and precision. And she has long dark hair and very nice legs, but that's neither here nor there.

Incidentally, there's no point knocking yourself out trying to pronounce her name. You can't, at least not her first name. It's Dutch, and the double Os conspire to form a sound not found in English, something midway between *oh* and *oo*. Say *KOHshuh VANderbeck* and you'll be close enough.

She stopped in the center of the room and looked at me. "Haven't you forgotten something?"

"Let's see . . . you're not wearing a coat, so I haven't forgotten to offer to take it. Your birthday's in November, so I haven't forgotten to send a card. We're not married, so I haven't forgotten our anniversary . . ."

"Dinner," she said. "Tonight," she said. "The French Café, six-thirty, my treat," she said. "Honestly, Nebraska, I can understand your forgetting about me, the time, and the place, but forgetting a free dinner . . . that's not like you, my friend."

"You can say that again. I'm sorry. It just slipped my mind entirely."

"Mm. That was my guess. I hope your absent-mindedness is due to an almost total immersion in your new book and not to another woman."

That stung. It hit a little close to home.

I said, "Truth is, another woman has distracted me."

She let one eyebrow climb slightly skyward.

"The French Café this ain't, but if you're hungry I'll throw together something for us and tell you about her."

Which is what I did.

Some time later we were in the back room, in my office, which doubles as my bedroom. When not folded out, the fold-out sleeper sofa leaves plenty of room for desk, chair, typing stand, dresser, and other necessities. When folded out, the sofa leaves slightly less room than an ant needs to jitterbug in, but one learns to make do.

I was on my back, watching the ceiling go black. Koosje was on her side, using my left shoulder as a pillow. Her breath was cool against the side of my neck.

She said, "Why did you tell me?"

I said, "Because you have a right to know."

"No, I don't." Her lips moved against my shoulder. "Not

a *right*. We don't have that kind of arrangement. If you want to go to bed with another woman, it doesn't have anything to do with me."

"It does," I said. "Because of the way I feel about you. Because of the way I think you feel about me."

Koosje rolled away from me and groped for her glasses on the far arm of the sofa. They were wide-lensed designer glasses, "eyewear," as they say in the trade, and they made her look very studious and intellectual, even if she was stark naked, with her hair going every direction.

"I've never made any claim or demand on you. I wouldn't."

"I know," I said. "That doesn't change anything. My wanting to be faithful comes from me, not you. Old-fashioned word, faithful."

Koosje elbowed herself into a sitting posture and rested her head against the back of the sofa. "Mm. A good word, I think." She looked at me. "If things had . . . progressed last night, would you have gone to bed with her?"

"I don't know. Probably. I'd like to think not, but probably. There's no denying events were heading that direction. Maybe I possess such inner strength as would have caused me to bring things to a screeching halt if put to the test . . . but I doubt it. Not that I feel compelled to hop on everything that's hot and hollow, as Hammett so eloquently phrased it—"

"Charming."

"—I think I'm a *little* more sentient than that. But there's a whole lot of . . . *something* left over between Carolyn and me, even after all these years. The flood of memories, of emotions, all of which I thought I'd put behind me years ago—it's practically overwhelming."

"Mm," Koosje said. She says that a lot. It had taken me a while to deduce that it's just a habit, just a reflex, just a little sound she makes that doesn't necessarily mean anything at all. She drifted out of the room, and a few seconds later I heard her moving about in the bathroom.

Then there was the soft tap of bare feet on the kitchen linoleum, the dull, sucking *pook!* of the refrigerator door opening, and the rattle of cans on the fridge's wire shelves. A moment later she ambled back through the doorway with two Falstaffs.

"That's what I call a vision," I said. "A naked maiden bearing beer."

"Hardly 'maiden,' " she said. She crawled across the rumpled sheets and handed me a can. I pried back the pull tab and she did likewise.

"Here's to crime," I said.

"Here's to crime fiction," she corrected, tapping the edge of her can against the edge of mine. "You know, what you're feeling isn't unusual," she said, settling back again. "People aren't machines. We can't turn emotions on and off like a spigot, nor would we want to. When a relationship ends, there are bound to be feelings left, good or bad, and the people who were involved have to learn to handle those feelings. Some are easier than others. When a love affair ends naturally, when it runs its course, then it's easier. There's a certain mutual agreement that it's time to end things—or put them on different terms."

" 'Can't we just be friends?' "

"Exactly. But when one party wants to end the relationship before the other is ready . . ." she shrugged and sipped beer. "Unfortunately, it happens that way more often than not. From what you tell me, that's what happened with you and Carolyn. She left you holding the bag, so to speak, without offering any real explanation. The story never had an ending, happy or otherwise. Whether you know it or not, you've probably been waiting, wanting, to write an ending to that chapter for twenty years."

I rested a hand on the inside of her left knee. "So what do you prescribe, doctor?"

She looked at me. It was hard to see her, since the room had grown so dark. "I can't decide for you. What do *you* want?"

"Well, that's easy. I want to go to bed with Carolyn. And then when I wake up the next morning I want it never to have happened. I want to have my cake and eat it too—"

"Bad analogy."

"I see your point. But do you see mine? Is it unreasonable to want it both ways?"

"Unreasonable, no. Impossible, yes. Face it, Nebraska, if you're going to have a relationship with Carolyn Longo, or anyone else, then you'll have to accept whatever consequences it may have on the other relationships in your life."

"Right now I'm only concerned about *one* other. What consequences?"

Koosje ran the sweating beer can across her forehead and down one cheek. The room had been warm to start with, and we hadn't helped it cool off any. Windows, such as they were, were a narrow strip of glass and aluminum high up on the back wall. If the wind was from the east, great. If not, no ventilation. The apartment had air-conditioning, a window unit crammed into a hole cut into the living-room wall, but it didn't seem to do much besides make noise and run up the electric bill.

"I don't know," Koosje said. "I honestly don't. I've never asked you to be faithful to me, but I'm pleased that you have been." She gripped my arm. "If you weren't . . . Well, I don't know. Speaking as the cold, clinical professional—"

"I've never known you to be either cold or clinical."

"Mm, maybe we'll try that game later on. At any rate, the professional answer is, 'We're not married, we've made no promises, we have no hold on one another. We don't know how long our relationship will last, or whether it's strong enough to survive external buffets, or whether it should continue if it isn't.' "

"All right. And *not* speaking as the cold, clinical professional?"

She looked at me. Her face was very close to mine, but

I could barely see it in the diffuse gray light. Her voice was a whisper, a soft ghost of a whisper in the darkened room. "What we've got is good, very good. Do we really want to risk losing it?"

I held her close. After a while, I held her very close. And, once again, she was neither cold nor clinical.

CHAPTER
FIVE

Loverboy, a.k.a Jonathon Desotel, got the next morning off: I had bigger fish to fry, or at least different ones. So I let him find his own way to work, and by seven-fifteen I was back at Hascall Street, or what was left of it. The crew was beginning to assemble. The foreman had told me work started at seven-thirty.

At seven-forty I saw Al Patavena's Stud Baker pull onto Vinton Street and park along the curb, opposite where it had stood yesterday. Patavena, behind the wheel, was alone. That was okay: I had wanted to try to undo yesterday's damage by interviewing them separately today. But it was kind of an interesting development, since yesterday the two had seemed as inseparable as Willie and Joe.

Patavena paused a little when he caught sight of me, in the alley that connected Hascall and Vinton behind the church and school buildings. But he put on a resolute face and kept coming, ignoring me as he passed.

As he passed, I said, "Where's your boyfriend," not only to get the conversational ball rolling but also because, even at that hour of the day, a little bit of strategy was beginning to jell in the old gray matter.

Patavena stopped, turned, glowered. "Keep your mouth shut, prick. Or I'll shut it for you."

Of the two—Abel and Patavena—Patavena stood the better chance of making good on the gangsters-movie threat. He was skinny but in that rangy, wiry way that you have to watch. Still, I didn't think we'd come to blows, and even if we did, I always had my master plan to fall back on: fight dirty, then run.

I shrugged carelessly. "Hey, what do I care what two consenting gardenias do in the privacy of their own hovel? I just hardly recognized you without your shadow, that's all."

Patavena's glower deepened. He didn't know what exactly I meant by it, but he didn't think he liked it. His eyes were hot. "He didn't feel too good today," he grumbled. "We hit the bottle pretty hard last night."

"A little celebration, maybe."

"Payday yesterday."

I laughed. "Okay. If you say so."

He had turned and taken half a step toward joining the others. Now he stopped and looked at me again. "What's that supposed to mean—if I say so?"

I smiled and looked away from him, toward a line of poplars that sheltered a house from the alleyway. "If I were you, I'd be real interested in finding out if Abel is really home with a case of bottle fatigue right about now, or . . ." I ended it with a shrug that was supposed to be worldly-wise.

Patavena moved closer. "Or what? Spit it out, shitface."

"Your buddy-boy got awful quiet yesterday when we started talking about Longo's girl, didn't he? I think that's interesting. I think maybe the cops don't know Longo had action going on the side. So if Longo had a wad of dough to stash, and he stashed it with the girlfriend . . ."

"Hell," Patavena said hotly.

"Good hiding place, but inaccessible. What I'm getting

at is you and Abel might be the only guys who know about this woman. If she's still around town, that is. Suppose Abel figured that out yesterday. Suppose he managed to figure out that seventy-eight thousand divided by two is only thirty-nine thousand but seventy-eight thousand divided by one is seventy-eight thousand. Suppose he started looking for a time when he could ditch you and hit on the girlfriend by himself, like . . ."

Patavena was silent a moment. Beads of sweat appeared on his face, but then it was a muggy day. I waited while the gears turned. Like the mills of God, they moved slowly, but they moved. After a minute or so, he looked at me with the menacing scowl back in place.

"Bullshit, man," he spat. "Marlon wouldn't pull nothin' like that, not on me. We been through a lot, him and me, and if he was gonna rip me off, he's had lots of chances."

"Seventy-eight thousand of them?"

"Fuck you. 'Sides . . . Marlon don't got any car."

With that he turned again and this time successfully walked away from me.

I trudged back up the hill to my crate and moved it down Seventy-fourth to where it and Vinton conspire to form a concrete T. I had a good view of Patavena's car when he got into it not five minutes later.

He roared off down the hill. I followed.

I followed him to Ralston, a bedroom community just south of Omaha. I followed him through a couple of picture-post-card neighborhoods, keeping well back when we left heavy traffic. I followed him to an Amoco where he consulted a phone book at a drive-up booth. And then I followed him to a mobile-home park that we had done a good job of circling but not stumbling across for the past half hour.

After a little searching, Patavena brought the clunky car to a jerky stop in front of a trailer at the edge of the park, alongside a faded red Le Car. The trailer—I know they

don't call them that anymore, but what the hell—the trailer
was pastel green with white trim and green-and-white metal
awnings. Three wooden steps, redwood stained, took you
up to a narrow white metal door. Someone had been doing
some landscaping on the little strip of lawn surrounding
the home, white marble chips covering the ground around
the skirt of the place in a loping, curved outline that ran
from about eighteen inches at its narrowest point to maybe
three feet at its widest. A couple of puny evergreen bushes
in the middle of the decorative stones wilted in the glare
of the morning sun. Two bags of marble chips slouched
against the trailer's side. The idea of trying to beautify such
unbeautiful surroundings struck me as both futile and touching.

I let the Impala coast to a stop under some maples and
watched Patavena fly out of his wagon and up the wooden
steps. He pounded on the door and it opened. I couldn't
see who operated it from the inside. I couldn't hear what
Patavena said. But it was good enough to get him admitted.

As the trailer door slammed, I reached across and opened
my car's glove compartment. Inside, I keep an old canvas
bag, the kind banks used to give you. Inside that I keep
one of my two .38 police revolvers. I don't like automatics.
The more sophisticated something is, the greater the possibility of a breakdown. If you're in a situation that calls for a
gun, you want to be able to pull the damn trigger without
having to wonder whether or not it'll do any good.

I shook out the gun, checked the cylinder, climbed out
of the car, and stuffed the gun into my back pocket. I know
us hardboiled private-eye guys are supposed to shove our
guns into our waistbands, and our untucked shirttails are
supposed to hide them, but anyone who's tried that trick
knows it gets mighty uncomfortable mighty fast, and a shirt-
tail hides a pistol about as well as a veil hides a stripper.

I went across the little pea-stone road, climbed the stairs,
and cocked my head toward the door. Voices came from

within, but indistinctly. A small air conditioner jammed into a window alongside the door did a good job of drowning out everything.

I hit the aluminum with the flat of my hand and didn't have to wait too long for the door to be opened. The doorman was a woman, a trim, dark-haired woman of twenty-seven, twenty-eight.

"Hi there," I said. "Would you be interested in taking out a subscription to *Real Thrilling Crime Detective Stories?*"

She opened her mouth, but nothing came out. No words, that is, only sound, a sort of *ehhhhh.*

Then Marlon Abel stepped out from behind the door. He made sure I saw the .22 he held.

"Get in here, cop," he hissed.

Nobody ever calls me shamus.

I got in there, edgewise, so as not to reveal the gun butt sticking out of my back pocket.

The mobile home was like the time machine on *Doctor Who*, bigger on the inside than on the outside. That was the first thing I noticed. The second thing I noticed was that the place was a mess. Not messy, but a mess, a wreck. Someone, Marlon Abel, no doubt, had tossed the joint, torn it apart looking for something. I could guess what.

I didn't notice too much else. I was preoccupied with the gun that was rudely staring at me from Abel's hand.

"The guy with the firepower usually gets to do the talking," I said.

"Then shut up."

"Take care of him, Marlon." Patavena. I hadn't noticed him, slouched in a far corner of the living room. His face was red and veins stood out in his neck and forehead. He held a wooden duck, a decorative duck decoy, between his wide hands, as if he'd like to twist the bird's head off. No doubt I'd interrupted a fiesty discussion of how Marlon came to be on the premises without his old buddy Al.

"You shut up too," Abel said. He eyed me a long minute,

blinking rapidly several times. The one-eyed monster staring at me never blinked.

"All right," Abel finally announced, as if we'd been having a discussion. "All right." A glance, only that, at Patavena. "Don't just stand there. Go finish the bedroom."

"We ain't done talkin'."

"We sure the fuck are. Finish the goddamn bedroom."

Patavena threw the decoy into a cushionless chair, from which it bounced onto the carpet. The tall man's Adam's apple bobbed a couple of times before he spoke: "Yeah, I'll go finish the goddamn bedroom. But you and me, we ain't done yet. We still gotta talk about how you fucked me over."

"I never fucked you over, stupid."

"Yeah, well, you were gonna."

"Bullshit." Abel was trying to keep the gun and his attention on me while carrying on a conversation with Patavena, far to his left. It wasn't easy. I didn't sympathize.

"Bullshit," Patavena replied hotly. "Then what'choo do, you borrow old man Steinhauer's car and come down here without me. I s'pose, you find the money, you're gonna come get me so we can split it."

"That's right, pinhead." Again he glanced at Patavena; again it was for only a second.

The reply seemed to suck the wind out of Patavena's jets. His mouth opened, closed, opened again, and said, "Oh. Uh."

"Now will you go finish the goddamn bedroom!" Sweat beaded Abel's forehead, even though he was standing right in front of the air conditioner. He dragged his left paw across his sort-of mustache and sniffed loudly.

Patavena hesitated, then went. The trailer layout was linear. The door opened to the living room, the living room segued into a minuscule kitchen, the bedroom was just past the refrigerator. It was from the bedroom that bumping, scraping, clunking noises now emerged.

"Jesus," the young woman at my right muttered under her breath.

"Saves," I said. She looked at me. "These guys friends of yours?" I said.

She snorted derisively.

"You two shut up," Abel said.

"I never said anything, asshole" the woman said.

"Well, shut up anyway."

"Fuck you. You think that gun makes you a big man."

"Excuse me," I said, "but the gun does make him a big man."

A loud crash came from the back room.

"Christ, he's trashing the place!" The woman took two steps forward. Abel's arcing the gun a few degrees toward her put a stop to that.

"You give us what we want, he'll quit."

"I told you, creep—I don't have any money."

The short, square man looked at me. I shrugged.

The bedroom door came open, and Patavena stepped out.

"Find anything?" Abel growled.

"Nah. 'Cept lookit this weird shit she got." He raised both arms. From one hand dangled a pair of manacles, black leather cuffs linked by six or eight inches of nickel chain. In the other hand he held a short but businesslike riding crop, also black. "Weird, huh?" Patavena said with an idiotic grin.

I glanced at the woman. Her face was impassive. I said, "It's bad manners to go prowling around in peoples' closets, especially lady peoples'. You didn't find what you're looking for; why not blow—go home and cry in each other's arms, or whatever you two like to do."

Abel brought back his right hand, meaning to caress the side of my head with the gun. It was a mistake. In that interval the gun was aimed at the ceiling, not me, and I didn't care so much about the ceiling getting ventilated. I spun a quarter turn on my right foot and brought my left knee up, hard, between his legs. He wilted and I took the noisemaker away from him with no trouble.

Patavena hadn't moved. He still stood in the semihallway formed by the outside wall and the fridge. He still held the woman's little playthings like trophies. He still wore an idiotic expression. But he was no longer grinning.

I said, "At risk of repeating myself, Laverne, take Shirley here and blow."

"Uh," he said. "We got two cars."

"Typical American family. For cryin' out loud, I didn't kill him. He'll be all right in two or three minutes. In three or four minutes you had both better be well on your way to far away from here." I waggled the gun. Patavena stepped forward, remembered he had the toys, and pressed them on me. I took them both in my left hand, making a big deal of keeping Abel's gun aimed at Patavena's belly. Not that I needed the piece anymore. The fight had gone out of them.

Abel, groaning, gagging, was almost upright again, thanks in part to a nearby armchair. Patavena, when he had deposited his burden on me, moved to help him. They staggered out of the metal house. Neither looked back.

I closed the door after them and shot the bolt.

"Shiiit," the woman breathed when the door was shut. She picked her way across the ruined room and sat on a love seat whose cushions were . . . well, elsewhere. She rummaged around and through some junk on the floor, came up with cigarettes and a throwaway lighter, and fired up. Her hands trembled, but barely.

I got my first real look at her then. Slender, dark haired—as I've said. Well-built in that stripped-down, athletic sort of way. Built for speed. She looked familiar, and in a minute I knew why. Add ten years and the concomitant little wrinkles, sags, and bulges, and you'd have Carolyn Longo. I wondered if Gregg Longo had realized the resemblance between his new cookie and the old model. Had it been coincidental? Or had it been the point?

When she had taken a deep drag of smoke and released it in a shaky exhalation, I pronounced my name.

"Eloise Slater," she said with a vague cigarette-hand gesture toward herself. "Thanks for getting rid of those two."

"No charge."

"By the way, don't you think you'd better look and see if they really left?"

"They left."

"They could be out there waiting for you. Or me." She pulled again on the gasper.

"They're not," I said.

Eloise Slater narrowed her eyes to peer at me through the cigarette smoke. "Yeah? Well . . . I'm from Missouri." With a movement so quick it was barely a movement at all, she angled herself off the love seat, dodged the debris on the floor between her and the door, and pulled back the little brass-plated bolt. She hesitated, stuck the cigarette between her lips, opened the door two inches, maybe less, and looked out. When that proved nonfatal, she opened the door wide enough to take her head and shoulders and gave the unpaved road outside a thorough going-over.

"What part of Missouri?" I said.

She closed the door and bolted it. "Wise-ass," she breathed, a slight, rueful smile at her lips. The smile tightened as her eyes left my face and took in the little room. "Geez, they trashed the place."

"No permanent damage," I said. "These guys were strictly amateurs, and bad amateurs at that. Pros don't content themselves with looking under furniture. They take the furniture apart, they pull the paneling off the walls, they rip up the carpets, they generally make like a plague of locusts. Incidentally . . ." I held out the crop and the manacles. "Yours, I believe."

She took them. Her face was open and, except for that faint smile at her full lips, expressionless. "Don't knock it till you've tried it," Eloise Slater said.

"What makes you think I haven't?" Her left eyebrow

rose slightly, speculatively. I said, "Is that what Gregg Longo came here for?"

She drew again on the cigarette. "You make me sound like a hooker. I'm not. Gregg and I were—well, I don't know if you'd say we were in love, but we liked each other. A lot. I was sorry when he got killed, real sorry. I miss him. And if we . . . played our little games, what's it to you or anybody? And what in hell's going on around here, anyway? First those two comedians and now you."

"The cops, local and federal, think Longo knocked over a bunch of banks earlier this summer."

"I know. I watch the news."

"Then you know that he—or whoever—made a tidy profit on the venture. When Longo was killed he didn't have any loot in his back pocket or in the car." Not true: He had that stolen fifty, but as Carolyn had said, it could have come from anywhere. Including Gregg Longo's hidden stash, if he was the thief. "The authorities didn't find any in his house," I went on. "His wife doesn't have it. Abel and Patavena, the two charmers you've been entertaining this morning, they don't have it. As they proved by coming here in the belief that Longo might have parked the cash with you."

"Boy, did someone steer them wrong. If I had seventy-eight thousand bucks would I be living in a coffin like this and spending six nights a week at the Grain Bin lounge working for pennies an hour plus tips plus all the ass-pinching I can stand?"

Depends how shrewd you are, I thought, but didn't voice it. "The cops never talked to you after Longo was killed?"

"Hey, I don't mean to sound ungrateful or anything, but what's it to you?"

"I'm a private detective, hired to investigate Longo." It was all she needed to know. "The cops. They never talked to you?"

"No, thank you. I guess they don't know about me and

Gregg. I didn't think anybody did. On account of him being married, you know? Anyhow, I wasn't too broken up that the cops didn't come hassle me."

"I don't suppose. But didn't it occur to you that you might be able to clear Longo?"

"How?" She sucked on the cigarette. "He didn't hide any money here, but that wouldn't prove he didn't hide it somewhere else."

"You work nights. That means you saw Longo during the day." She nodded. "These were daylight robberies. If Longo was with you on any or all of those occasions—"

"What, you think I wrote it down in my diary every time he shot his load? If he was over here every day, sure, I'd go tell the cops that. But he wasn't . . . and dates, I don't know any dates. I'd end up getting hauled through the grinder by the cops, and it wouldn't do Gregg any good. Wouldn't do him any good anyway, 'cause he's dead."

Unassailable logic. I said, "How long were you and Longo . . ."

"About four, five months, up until he got killed. I met him at the bar. He was there with those other two lowlifes, whatever you said their names were, which I guess is how they knew about me. They didn't ever come around more than once, twice. Never after me and Gregg took up."

I righted a chrome-and-vinyl kitchen chair and sat on it backward. "What do you think, was your boyfriend the bank-robbing type?"

She had wandered back across the room and resumed her place on the love seat. "I don't know what 'type' that is," she said. "Maybe he was and maybe he wasn't. But I don't think he did."

"Did he ever say anything, do anything that made you wonder?"

"Like what?"

"Like I don't know. Maybe something that didn't register at the time. But then he got killed, and they were saying he robbed those banks, and you sort of said to yourself, 'Holy cow, that's what he meant.' Anything?"

"Well . . ."

I waited.

"This is so stupid . . . I mean . . ." She made a disgusted sound, put on a face to go with it, and said, "Look, once he said how he ought to go rob a bank or knock over a liquor store or something. You know, because he was so strapped for money. But it was just something you say, you know?"

I knew. People say things all the time. "If X did Y I'll kill him." "If things go on like this I'll jump off a building." "If I don't get a job pretty soon I'm gonna have to start robbing banks." Ninety-nine times out of a hundred it's just talk. Contrary to the TV mystery shows, cops are usually hip enough to know that. They also know, and so did I, that there's always that one time in a hundred.

I said, "Well, how did he say it. I mean, did he just say it—'They want six hundred bucks to fix the car, and I don't have it unless I go rob a bank'—or did he have a plan?"

She looked at me through the gauze of smoke that rose from her mouth. "Get serious."

"I am serious."

"Well, hell no, he didn't have a plan. For cryin' out loud."

"Money was a problem for him the whole time you knew him?"

"Problem? Nah, how could it be? He didn't have any." She pulled on the cigarette. "I mean, yeah, sure he had money, a couple of bucks maybe. But nothing to spread around. Enough to buy a pack of cigarettes, not enough to make the rent. You know what I mean?"

"Believe me, I do. There was never a time when all of a sudden he seemed pretty flush, maybe had a couple extra bucks to spend?"

"If he did, he was cagey. Real cagey. When he died he still owed me a hundred bucks."

"Let's say he was cagey. Let's say he took care of those banks and he kept it from his wife and his pals and you—everybody. What would he do with the money? Where would he stash it?"

"How the hell would I know? I wasn't married to the guy. But I guess that wouldn't make any difference, since you say his wife doesn't know either. I liked Gregg a lot but I didn't know everything there was to know about him. I guess maybe we never had that kind of time to spend together, you know what I mean?"

This time I didn't know and said so.

Eloise Slater's eyes turned reminiscent. They were dark eyes, dark like Carolyn's, but where Carolyn's were almost black, Eloise's were gray, a dark gray, a gray-flannel gray. "When you spend a lot of time with someone, you talk, you know, about all kinds of things. When you don't have a lot of time, you don't want to waste it."

"You get down to business."

"There you go again, like I'm some kind of whore." There was neither anger nor resentment in her tone. There was, literally, nothing. "Well, think what you like. Gregg and me, we just had some nice times together. He wasn't perfect, but he was a really nice guy."

"Whips and chains notwithstanding."

She eyed me coolly. "You got it backward, mister."

"Really? I didn't know Longo very well, but I'd've never figured him for the type."

Eloise Slater crushed her cigarette into a lime-green plastic ashtray she found under the loveseat. "You and your 'types.' There aren't any 'types.' Some people like some things and some people don't, and those are the only 'types' there are. You can't tell by looking. And a lot of people don't know what they like until they try. Gregg didn't know. Maybe you don't know either." Her eyes narrowed. "Maybe you'd like to try some things." She had placed the toys next to her on the love seat. Now she raised the cuffs.

The nickel chain caught the light and threw it back at me. "Maybe you'd like to try these on for size. Maybe you'd like for me to tie you spread-eagle with a gag in your mouth and a leather hood over your head." She grinned. "Would you like that?"

"Thanks for the offer, but never before lunch."

She shrugged with studied nonchalance. Most people shrug with their shoulders. "You may not know what you're missing."

"And then again I may." The tank top and cutoffs she wore did little to mask the pleasures her lithe body might hold. Might, hell.

Again she shrugged, and dropped the cuffs. "Maybe you do. Anyhow, I don't know what else I can tell you. About Gregg, I mean. If he was a crook he sure kept it hidden from me. If he had seventy-eight thousand he sure didn't leave it with me. He didn't leave anything. Except a toothbrush." She looked around at the disarray. "You're welcome to search the place, if you can find the place."

"I'll pass on that offer too. I don't think Abel and Patavena will bother you anymore. But if they do, or if you think of anything that may be helpful—something Longo said, maybe, or did—give me a call." I handed her one of my business cards. She studied it as if she expected it to reveal more than my name, rank, and telephone number.

"Maybe I'll call sometime," she said after a long while.

CHAPTER
SIX

I'm a suspicious kind of guy. Goes with the territory, maybe, although it's a chicken-egg situation: Am I a suspicious kind of guy because of the trade I've plied, with varying degrees of enthusiasm, for so many years? Or have I been drawn to my various investigation-oriented jobs because I was a suspicious kind of guy to start with?

In any event, there I was, being suspicious, in my car, just down the road from where the mobile-home court's entrance emptied into the street. I was parked on a side street half a block away, in the shade of a two-story sand-colored medical-arts building, listening to the radio and keeping an eye on the gravel drive leading into the trailer park.

Half an hour later, give or take, a once-red Le Car appeared at the end of the drive in a cloud of dust, made a right turn without signaling and, a few blocks down, another right onto the high road. I didn't get a good look at the driver—too much white dust from the trailer park's gravel lot—but the car was Eloise Slater's.

There were any number of reasons for her to head out into the wide world. A varied selection of them went through my head as I followed her down that ribbon of highway, as the bard has it. Most of them were perfectly innocent. I followed her anyway.

I followed her over to Seventy-second Street, followed her north and into the city. She turned left at the light at Grover Street. For an instant I thought she was heading for the construction site on Hascall and wondered what the heck for. But she turned left again immediately, into the Howard Johnson lot. I drove on by, turned right at the next opportunity, got onto the access road that runs parallel to Seventy-second, and doubled back down to the light. By the time I pulled into the HoJo, the Le Car was parked and empty, its occupant just entering the glass doors to the coffee shop.

The coffee shop was the squeaky-clean vinyl-and-plastic palace these places always are. I grabbed a two-top booth near the front windows, which afforded me a good view of the back of Eloise Slater's head and the front of her companion's. He was a light-skinned black man in a sharp black pin-striped suit, red silk tie, and blindingly white shirt. His hair was medium-long and shiny, worn in the wet-looking "curl" that is Michael Jackson's major contribution to Western civilization. I couldn't hear much of their exchange— the rest of the clientele lacked the courtesy to shut up while I was trying to eavesdrop—just a few snatches, meaningless out of their context: Eloise thanking him for meeting her, him saying it was no problem, Eloise saying he was looking good, him returning the compliment. You get the idea. When she sat down and they began discussing whatever it was they were discussing, I could hear nothing. And my lip-reading isn't good enough to have deciphered the black fellow's side of the conversation.

When the waitress ambled over, I told her I'd changed my mind and just needed a coffee to go. Then I sat in my car and slurped burned brown water from a plastic container and shuttled across the AM band before giving up with a disgusted switch-off of the radio and the silent promise to invest in a tape deck.

Forty minutes later, Eloise Slater and her friend appeared. They stood on the walk in front of the motel for a few minutes, then she climbed into her car, and he got behind the wheel of a gray Chcvy Celebrity Eurosport. The only outward distinction between a Eurosport and a plain old ordinary garden-variety Celebrity seems to be the red pin-stripe on the black vinyl bumperstrip around the car. I won-dered how much extra the pinstripe cost. Wondered idly, as I jotted the car's license number on the side of my coffee container.

The Grain Bin had been aptly named. The bar-and-steak house was tucked into an old grain-elevator operation west of Ralston. The elevator itself, long disused, towered over the flat beige cement-block building that housed the bar and restaurant. The old elevator was a tall stainless-steel rectangle. Resting as it did on the perfectly flat plain, it could be seen for miles in any direction and looked like nothing so much as a defiant finger thrust against the hazy midwestern sky. "The Grain Bin" was stenciled in red, at about a forty-degree angle, across the front of the elevator.

I had followed Eloise Slater far enough to feel reasonably confident she was heading home, then peeled off onto the county highway that brought me to the steak house. Oddly, Eloise's going home struck me as intriguing, not innocuous. She is held at gunpoint while two lunatics tear her home apart. A private investigator questions her about her involve-ment with a married man who very possibly was a bank robber. Then she hops in her car and drives off to have coffee with a friend. Then she goes home. Strange sequence. You'd think she'd either stay home and try to put the place back together, or clear out and stay the hell away until she got her head screwed on again.

As I said, intriguing.

I pulled off the highway into the Grain Bin's unpaved lot.

Once upon a time this had probably been a hotbed of

agricultural activity, but the expansion of the city and its bedroom towns had pushed the farming frontier ever farther back. When I was a kid, my uncle used to take us for drives in the country—country that is now practically central Omaha. The Grain Bin, in its original incarnation, had once been isolated out here on the prairie, connected to the rest of the world only by a couple of narrow roads and a railroad siding. Now it sat at the intersection of a state highway and a main county road, territory it shared with a truck stop, a petroleum depot, and the Cloud 9 Motel ("Phone In Every Room").

The long beige building was fronted by a rustic boardwalk-and-eaves arrangement—you know, the kind you used to see on *Gunsmoke*. The wild-West effect was spoiled by neon signs indicating Lounge and Restaurant over the appropriate rough-hewn doors.

I yanked open the door under the buzzing Lounge sign and entered.

And was struck blind.

So, at least, it seemed, although after a few moments my eyes adjusted to the extreme blackness of the bar. I've always thought it strange that bars, where people are liable to consume alcohol, which is apt to interfere with people's navigational abilities, are always darker than hell on a moonless night. But they are, and the Grain Bin Lounge was no slouch in that department. When my eyes came back on duty, I could see that the place was one large room dominated by a large horseshoe-shaped bar. The rest of the floor space was given over to tables and booths. Against the far wall, behind the bar, four or five pinball and video machines stood blinking and glowing mutely. Directly above them was a loft, or mezzanine, constructed of the same rough wood as the building's façade.

The bar was quiet. There were maybe half a dozen custom-ers in the joint, two at the bar, sitting apart, the rest scattered here and there, intent on their own business. Faint country

music and the fainter aroma of barbecue sauce drifted from
the direction of the restaurant, getting ready for the lunch
trade.

I stepped over to the bar and sat near the cash register.
The stools were high with low backs. The bar was ringed
with a roll of black padded vinyl. I climbed onto a stool
and rested my elbows on the vinyl and waited for the bartender.

The bartender was a woman, twenty-five or thirty—the
older I get, the harder it is for me to judge—with sad eyes
that didn't go with the round, freckled, little-girl face. She
was ten, fifteen pounds overweight, but she had the kind
of build that can take it and make good use of it. She wore
a new T-shirt, green with a white sea gull stenciled over
the left breast, khaki pants, three gold earrings, two in the
left lobe, one in the right, and a serpentine gold chain at
her throat.

"What'll it be?" Making the effort to be pleasant.

"I'm looking for a girl."

She laughed and looked dubiously at me.

"Let's rephrase that: I'm looking for a *specific* girl. Eloise
Slater. I was told she worked here." That was true; I had
been told by Eloise.

"Well . . ."

I went for the wallet and showed her the permit. "I'm a
private investigator, working for a lawyer." All true. "There's
a possibility that Ms. Slater might have some money coming
to her . . ." Also true—I mean, for all I knew, she *did*
have money coming to her, a tax refund or something. It's
usually a good idea to cleave to these Chinese-fortune-cookie
sorts of statements in situations such as this. Outright lies
have a nasty tendency to come back and bite you in the
backside later on.

"Really?" the freckle-faced kid said, and now her eyes
went with the face. "How much money?"

"I don't know that. They just give me names."

"Hang on." Freckles went and pulled a battered tin recipe box from a shelf beneath the register. She opened it, flipped through some index cards, and came over with one. The Slater woman's name, address, phone number, and Social Security number were neatly inked in green ballpoint on the lined card. I made a big deal of copying the info into my spiral notepad, although I already knew where she lived.

"You know Eloise, then, do you?" I said casually as I wrote.

"We work together sometimes. She usually works nights, and I've been working days lately on account of my boyfriend's on the day shift now, too, down at the—"

"It's nice you can arrange your hours to spend time with your boyfriend." Freckles smiled, a little shyly. "What about Eloise. She okay to work with?"

Freckles shrugged. "Yeah, sure, she's okay, you know."

"Shows up when she's supposed to, does her job, doesn't make trouble . . ."

"I guess so. Why d'you want to know?"

"It's important," I said. I tapped the notepad with my pen. "For the record." I winked conspiratorily.

"Oh. Sure. Well, *I* have no complaint with Eloise."

"That's good." I pretended to write it down. "You talked about your boyfriend . . . I wonder, is Eloise seeing anyone regularly?"

"Hang on." Freckles left to take care of one of the other men at the bar. I waited. Two fellows in pale-blue work shirts drifted in. The shirts bore the insignia of the oil company down the road. They found a booth across the room, took menus from the clip behind the salt and pepper rack, and studied the subject. Apparently lunch was served in the bar as well as the restaurant.

"Now what were you saying?" Freckles said, as she leaned against her side of the bar.

"Eloise Slater," I said. "Boyfriends?"

"Oh, yeah, that's right. Well, I don't know. I mean, I

know she goes out with guys, but I don't know if she has anyone steady, you might say. Every so often she'll come in a little late—five, ten minutes, no big deal, everybody does that sometimes—and say it was 'cause she was with a guy, but I don't know who or whether it's the same guy every time." She lifted the recipe card and tapped the edge of it against the bar a couple of times. "You got her address and phone number—why'n'cha ask *her* all this stuff?"

I smiled and folded my notepad and slid off the stool. Freckles turned to replace the card. "By the way," I said. "When does Eloise Slater work next?"

"Tonight," Freckles said without turning. "Six to two."

My eyes were knocked out again when I got outside, but I shoved them back into place and went to where I'd parked the Impala, in the shade of the grain elevator. At least, it *had* been shade. The sky had taken on a kind of purple-gray overcast since I'd seen it last, and the hard lines between sun and shadow were blurred.

I slid behind the wheel and glanced at my sketchy notes before flipping the notepad up onto the dash. Freckles had told me little I didn't already know and nothing that didn't jibe with what the Slater woman had told me herself—which was not necessarily a bad thing. I had no idea how, or whether, Eloise Slater fit into the equation. I had no idea yet what the equation *was*. Certainly Gregg Longo's friends and loved ones didn't completely dismiss the possibility that he *could* have knocked over those banks. But seventy-eight thousand dead presidents had yet to make their whereabouts known.

The irony of today's events did not escape me. I had done what Carolyn Longo first contemplated hiring me to do: I had found out whether her husband had been seeing another woman.

Now I had to think of a good way of telling her that the answer was yes. And there was no good way.

I slid the key into the ignition, but before I could start the engine, something cool and very solid insinuated itself against the back of my neck, behind and just below my right ear. I glanced at the rearview mirror and saw the top of Marlon Abel's head.

Three thoughts chased each other across the vacuum between my ears. The first was that I had taken Abel's peashooter away from him back at Eloise Slater's place and hadn't given it back. The second was that it was not impossible for Abel to own two guns, or to have acquired a new one in the past couple of hours. The third was that I had underestimated him, or overestimated myself. I had taken him and Patavena for a couple of short-hitters. It was now obvious that I had been mistaken. Painfully obvious.

"Shut the door," Abel said. "Let's go for a ride."

I shut the door, all right, but not until after I'd pitched myself out of the car and hit the dirt. Literally. Abel made a noise like a surprised yak and went to get out of the backseat, but as soon as he popped open the door I popped it shut again with a well-aimed kick. I was lying on my back next to the car, where I hoped the odds of getting shot were lower, so my mule kick had a lot of leverage behind it.

Abel's right wrist was caught between the car body and the window frame when the door swung back on him. He let out a howl of pain and dropped the eight-inch piece of threaded pipe he'd been holding. I kicked it under the car.

Twenty or thirty feet away, a door opened on Patavena's pitted Studebaker, and the man came out from behind the wheel. He carried an aluminum baseball bat.

I jumped up, dived back into the car, and hit the glove-compartment latch.

I got my hand on the canvas bag just as Patavena got his hand on my left ankle.

He yanked. I dropped the bag and made a grab for the

steering wheel as it slid by me. Missed. My right side and then my right shoulder banged hard against the doorstep and then against the unpaved lot as Patavena dragged me out.

He let go of me to get both hands around the bat, which he raised high overhead.

I crabbed under the car, groping for the pipe Abel had dropped. Found it. Snaked out from under the car on the far side.

Patavena was coming around the front end of the car, choking the metal bat in his right hand. The look on his face was funny—funny strange, I mean, not funny ha-ha. A wide-mouthed, wide-eyed, vacuous look. Empty. Emotionless. I've seen people look more animated going after a housefly.

I rolled up onto my feet, ducked as Patavena swung wide and missed, and, two-handed, whacked him with the pipe as hard as I could on the outside of his left knee.

He gurgled in pain and brought the bat down across my back.

It was lucky we were so close and he was so tall. The angle was such that what collided with my back was mainly Patavena's long, sinewy arms. The bat cracked my tailbone a good shot that soared up my spine like a bottle rocket, but the pain wasn't crippling. I took another swipe at the same knee and this time he went down.

I dived across the trunk of the car, went around Abel, who nursed his bent and bloody wrist, reached in for the canvas bag, and extracted the .38 I had so conscientiously put away before I left the trailer park. Better late than never.

Abel was making groany, gurgly noises that got louder when I grabbed his right wrist and squeezed it.

"Jesus Christ," he yelped, trying to pull away. Tears flooded his eyes and rolled down his cheeks, disappearing into the sparse vegetation on his lip. "Wha'j'a do that for?"

"To hurt you, stupid."

"Fuck, man, my wrist, I think it's broke."

"Remind me to stop at 7-Eleven and pick up a get-well card." I still held his wrist, but lightly. Now I gave it another squeeze, just a little one, just enough to make him wince and draw in a sharp breath. "Now, Marlon, why don't you tell me what the bright idea is."

"Man, I don't know wha—aaAAAHH! Stop it! All right, all right. Fuck . . ." He squeezed his eyes shut. Water dribbled out under the lids. I was touched. "We weren't gonna hurt you none."

"Oh dearie-dear, I must have overreacted again. Silly me. Too much caffeine, no doubt." I shoved the gun in his belly. "Can the sales talk, Abel. I'm not buying. I don't especially want your guts all over the backseat of my car, but I'm willing to live with it if need be. You get the idea?"

He nodded, weakly. "I don't feel so good."

"You feel better than you *will* if you don't tell me what I want to know. Why'd you two losers follow me? Why'd you jump me?"

On the other side of the car, Patavena was dragging himself upright. I ignored him. Abel was going into shock on me. His wrist probably was broken. It certainly was an attractive shade of blue.

"M-money," he said. His lips barely moved; they were rubbery looking, as if they were shot full of novocaine. "We thought . . . you and the girl . . ."

Abel pitched forward, and I two-stepped backward just in time to miss getting my shoes thrown up on.

Patavena was limping around the back of the car, still holding the bat. He stopped, looked at Abel sprawled on the ground, looked at me. "He dead?"

"No. Would you like him to be? I can arrange it." I lifted my right arm and let him see the gun. He dropped the bat. "What's the deal, Patavena? You figure the girl has the money and she and I came to some kind of arrangement after I shooed you boneheads away?"

"I guess . . ."

"You guess. Swell." Folks had started drifting over for lunch, and several of them wore that morbidly curious face you see on people driving past automobile wrecks. I said, "I ought to sic the cops on you two, just to get you out of my hair, but I can think of better ways to waste my time." I waved the gun at Abel, who was struggling to his hands and knees—*hand* and knees, I should say, since his right wrist couldn't have supported the weight of a hummingbird. "Take un-Abel here and get lost—again. This time I'm not kidding around. I don't like you guys anymore, and I don't want you hanging around me."

Patavena came and half-dragged, half-carried Abel to the Studebaker. I watched them leave. Then I did likewise.

CHAPTER
SEVEN

A not-too-much-younger me could easily have polished off an entire afternoon in a shopping mall, wandering around Crossroads or Westroads, playing looky-lou, checking things out, and generally being a nuisance for people bent on serious shopping. No more. Malls, all of them, give me the heebie-jeebies in my old age. I avoid them as much as is humanly possible, and when avoidance isn't humanly possible, I stick to my mission statement, in and out like a S.W.A.T. team. The only significant browsing I do takes place in bookstores. And the amount of time I spend on them has been decreasing in recent years, in proportion to the increasing amount of shelf space bookstores are wasting on videotapes, audiotapes, computer software, and other high-profit nonbook junk.

I mean, really—you go to a bookstore to look at *books*, right? You want video, audio, computer, you go to a video, audio, or computerstore.

Nevertheless, I made the obligatory pilgrimage to both B. Dalton and Waldenbooks when I hit Westroads. Dalton had The Book, my firstborn, in stock, two copies under Fiction and Literature, one under Mystery. Waldenbooks didn't carry it at all. I contemplated getting the kid behind the counter to special-order it for me and then never coming in to pick it up, but what would that accomplish? They'd only send it back to their jobber.

What I needed to do was special-order it for friends of mine who were too lazy or cheap to go do it themselves—leaving *their* names and telephone numbers with the clerk, of course.

Having ascertained that Dalton's inventory, at least, was up to standard, I stopped at Orange Julius and wolfed down a hot dog. I had missed lunch, having made a detour downtown after playing kiss-and-slap with Laurel and Hardy. Too late to tail Desotel to lunch, but I camped out across from the Olympic Club and picked him up as he came toddling back up the sidewalk shortly after one. Desotel had deviated from the routine in two respects: One, he was late. Usually he was back on duty by one at the latest. Two, he had company. Ordinarily he lunched alone and made the voyage to and from solo—except for me—but today he was accompanied by another man of Desotel's approximate height and build. From a block-and-a-half's distance, the view obstructed by the noontime crowd, that's about all I could tell. Desotel and the stranger paused on the sidewalk and presumably exchanged words, then the stranger jaywalked across the street and disappeared into the traffic and the crowd. Desotel continued up the sidewalk.

Desotel was in his mid-forties, a trim, good-looking fellow with wavy dark hair just going gray and a mustache trimmed to Wayne Newton specifications. He paused for a moment at the granite steps leading up to the club entrance, evidently deep in thought. Then he shook it off, grabbed the brass handrail, and hauled himself up the steps two at a time.

I waited a few minutes to make sure—reasonably sure—that Loverboy wasn't doing a double-back on me. When his blue blazer didn't come through the club's revolving doors again after fifteen minutes, I figured it was safe to head out to the mall.

Now, my hot dog nothing but a fond memory, I wandered downstairs to the basement level.

Westroads is basically a two-story mall, constructed around an open courtyard or lobby at the center. But there is a basement level that houses a few public establishments—a tailor, a dinner theatre, a couple of little offbeat shops that seem to change bimonthly—as well as mall offices, storage space, and other similarly scintillating attractions. Including the maintenance department.

I stopped in, asked for Lou Boyer, and was told he was supervising renovations being made to a space on the top level.

Back upstairs.

Lou Boyer had been a friend of Gregg Longo's. He had worked in Longo's contract maintenance business until it went out of business. Now he was an assistant-something-engineer for the outfit that owned the mall.

Down from J. C. Penney on the second level, in one of the few unoccupied retail spaces in the place, one of the workmen directed me to Boyer, an overweight, apple-cheeked fellow, with thin sandy hair on his head and a thick sandy walrus mustache under his nose. Lou Boyer stood under a tall wooden ladder, hollering instructions up to two men who were threading electrical conduit above the suspended ceiling. I picked my way over plastic drop cloths, around paint buckets, and between makeshift sawhorses to where he stood. I introduced myself, told him what I was doing. "Looks like they're keeping you busy," I said. The conversational approach.

"Never any problem with that." Boyer had a hoarse, Andy Devine kind of voice that suited him perfectly. "Old tenant moves out, new one moves in, and everything's got to be done yesterday. Hey, lookit, you're not supposed to be in here. The insurance . . ."

"Can we talk outside, then?"

Boyer ran a thumbnail over his mustache. "I s'pose . . . Hey, Steve! I'm gonna take a break for a minute."

We slid out from behind the opaque plastic curtains that pretended to keep the dust from drifting out into the mall, found an unoccupied bench near the Christian Science Reading Room, and sat.

"You workin' for Carolyn, then?" Boyer said. "Poor kid. Helluva way to lose a husband. Gotta be real tough on her."

"Real tough on Gregg, too."

Boyer grinned mirthlessly under the seaweed and pulled a pack of Wrigley's Spearmint from his shirt pocket. The Plen-T-Pack. He offered me a stick. I declined and watched him peel the foil paper from one and shove the gum into his mouth. "Well," he said around a chew. "I guess everything's a whole lot better for Gregg now, anyway."

That was open to discussion, but I didn't feel like discussing it. I said, "Carolyn's hired me because she wants to know one way or the other whether Gregg was guilty of what he's been accused of."

"No," Boyer said, chewing.

"No?"

He balled up the foil paper and shot it toward a trash bin eight feet away. Swish. "Not a chance Gregg knocked over those banks. Told the police the same thing, I did. Lookit—you know Gregg, did you?"

"Not really. By sight. We were in school together a long time ago."

"Uh-huh." He shifted the spearmint to the other side of his mouth. "Lookit, me and Gregg were in the service together. Navy. Now, the navy, it'll do one of two things for a guy who's maybe not a hunnert percent on the up-and-up. It'll either straighten him out good. Or it'll make him mean, mean like a snake."

"You're saying Longo cleaned up his act in the service."

"Yessir. Saw it with my own eyes. He came in a punk, a smart-mouthed little bastard who was too big for his britches. Not a bad sort, you understand, just a wise-ass. Could'a gone either way. The way he went, he came out a sailor. Not a saint; a sailor, someone who's learned some skills, picked up a little self-confidence, a little self-esteem, and maybe has something to look forward to now."

He looked at me. "I know what that means, and I know exactly what Gregg went through, in here"—he prodded his ample gut—"in the service. 'Cause I was just exactly the same as him when I upped, too."

"Okay. But cut to the present. Longo's out of work, his business has gone down the tubes, bills are piling up, his wife's killing herself working overtime to keep a roof overhead and bread on the table . . ."

He was shaking his head. "Doesn't matter. Doesn't matter. Gregg Longo would no more'a robbed a bank or a store or anything than you or I would. Just wasn't in him."

"Others who knew him aren't so sure."

"*Their* problem. Lookit, I knew the guy twenty years, on and off. Served with him, worked with him, worked *for* him." Again the gum migrated. "If he was a crook, wouldn't he'a tried to rip off his employees when the business started to go bad? He didn't. He didn't even cut anyone's pay or let anyone go until the very end. Maybe he should'a. But he didn't, and he didn't stiff his customers or his creditors or the tax man, none of that."

A large black woman shuffled by in a shapeless dress, rolled-down stockings, and carpet slippers. Boyer and I watched her push into the ladies' room just beyond the racks of pay phones.

Boyer said, "You ever notice how tough it is to tell a black lady's age? They go from like twenty to fifty, you don't know *how* old they are. The good-looking ones look real good and the not-so-good-looking ones look real bad, but you don't know how *old*. They hit fifty, and *bang!* everything falls apart kinda. Weird."

I said, "You were telling me how much Gregg Longo resembled Jimmy Stewart in *It's a Wonderful Life*."

He laughed. "Gregg was no Eagle Scout, nothing like that. He wouldn't go walkin' four miles in a blizzard to return four cents or whatever, like they say Abe Lincoln

did. Gregg had some problems. He was fond of the bottle.
He didn't mind an occasional bet. He had a roving eye—
you don't tell Carolyn I said that, now. And he never really
got unused to thinking his ship would come in."

"Oh?"

"Ah, you know, like somethin'd come up and he'd make
a million bucks and retire forever. Kid stuff. But Gregg
was an alright kind of guy and I'm sorry he's gone, and I'll
bet a week's pay he never robbed so much as a gum-ball
machine, much less a bank."

"Maybe he thought it was time to *make* his ship come
in."

Boyer fixed me with a long, hard look, interrupted only
by the rhythmic action of his fleshy jaw. "Well, god*damn*,
mister, if you're so all-fired sure Gregg's guilty like everyone
says, why're you takin' his widow's money to try and prove
he isn't?"

"I'm not trying to prove anything one way or the other,"
I said. "What I mean is, Carolyn didn't ask me to clear
him. She asked me to find out either way, so she can finally
get on with her life."

He looked at me some more. I had no idea I was so
interesting. "Uh-huh," he finally said. "Uh-*huh*. Well, you
asked me what I think and I told you. Lookit." He worked
the chewing gum some more. "Coupl'a days before he died,
Gregg paid me fifty bucks on a hunnert I borrowed him
back when I got this job. I mean, there I was working and
there he was with nothing, sort of. I told him it was a loan,
but of course I never expected to see it again—I mean,
I'd'a never asked him for it. But like I said, here he comes
with the fifty, apologizing 'cause he can't let me have the
whole hunnert. Now, if Gregg robbed those banks, he
could've afforded to let me have the whole hunnert. But
he probably wouldn't'a paid me at all, 'cause then he'd'a
been a *real* crook, see? Giving me just part of the money
he owed me, well, in my book that means the poor guy
was just another honest sucker down on his luck."

The logic was unassailable so I didn't assail it.

Boyer said, sidling up to it, "Way they were talking, a lot of money's missing."

I nodded. The authorities hadn't released an exact figure. "Almost eighty thousand."

"Well, there, then."

" 'There'?"

"Where's a guy like Gregg gonna stash eighty thousand bucks? In a Swiss bank?" He chuckled silently. "More like a paper carton in the basement."

"Between the local cops and the feds, all those kinds of things have been thoroughly checked. And dismissed."

"Well, there," Boyer repeated. He pushed himself off the bench and looked down at me. "I don't s'pose I helped you much. Or Carolyn, I oughta say."

I stood also. "Well, as I say, either way . . ."

"I don't s'pose you can really clear Gregg until they catch the guy who's really responsible. I mean, if they never find the money, they'll just assume Gregg hid it too good. That's too bad, 'cause the real guy probably figured the going was good when Gregg turned up as everybody's fall guy. He's probably catching rays on some tropical island right now. . . . Well, I better get back on the job. Already got laid off once this year, don't want to try for two. Nice talking with you."

I watched Boyer amble, Winnie-the-Pooh fashion, back to the plastic curtain. Then I went and fed a quarter to one of the public phones and called police headquarters. They put me on ignore for a week, then Kim Banner came on the line.

"Hey there, Sam Spade, I was just talking about you."

"Voice full of reverence, awe, and admiration, no doubt."

"Like usual. Listen, you know someone named Jurgenson, a fed?"

"I don't know any feds. I had a decent upbringing."

"Oh, yeah? What happened? Anyhow, I just spent about an hour on the phone with this character, playing twenty questions. Subject: a private license belonging to someone whose last name begins with *N* and rhymes with 'Nebraska.' "

"Huh. Bureau, or Treasury?"

"Treasury."

"Huh."

" 'Huh' isn't the word for it. Seems a little bird told this Jurgenson cat you're poking around into the Longo business, and Jurgenson doesn't like it."

"Jurgenson shouldn't listen to little birds."

"Funny, almost. What he doesn't like is *you* sticking your big fat nose into his investigation."

"My nose is neither big nor fat, and I haven't been sticking my big fat nose into anyone's investigation but my own. For all the good it's done. What's Jurgenson's beef? What'd he want to know?"

"Everything. Your history, your record, your reputation, your relations with the department . . ."

"He wants to know if I'm the type who'd disappear with seventy-eight thousand smackers if I happened to trip over them."

"Something like that."

"And you told him . . ."

". . . That I'm not sure *I* wouldn't disappear with seventy-eight thousand smackers if I tripped over them."

"Thanks, I'm sure that eased his mind a lot."

"Not as much as you might think. Listen, you getting anywhere on this thing?"

"Depends what you mean. What I'm getting is a lot of people who don't know anything one way or the other but wouldn't exactly be bowled over if they learned that Longo held up a bank or two in his spare time. Longo's got one staunch supporter, but he's outnumbered four to one by the people who *won't* stick their necks out and say they think it's impossible for Longo to have been a crook."

"Just like doctors recommending painkillers for people stranded on desert islands."

"Two of Longo's cronies in particular act like they think he *was* guilty. I hoped they'd lead me to the loot, but no luck. However, they did lead me to a little girlfriend Longo had. Seems she slipped between the bed and the wall, so to speak, during the investigation. Longo did such a good job of keeping her under wraps that no one knows about her. No one official. You might want to pass that along to whoever it should be passed along to. She's a member of the chorus—you know, 'Maybe he did, maybe he didn't, I don't know.' She says she didn't step forward because she can neither clear Longo nor implicate him. But maybe she knows more than she told me. Maybe she knows more than she knows."

"I'm just an officer of the law, that heavy philosophical shit is way too much for me. Gimme her name." I did. Over the wire I could hear the dull scratching of pencil on paper. "Right. Well, anything else you'd like me to do— pick up your laundry, feed the plants, water the cat . . ."

"This is what I get for being a good citizen and sharing what little I know with the local law-enforcement establishment—sarcasm. Well"—I worked a little quaver into my voice—"that's all right. Doing good is my reward. I don't need thanks."

"That's lucky," Banner said, and hung up.

I held the dead receiver until the dial tone came back. Then I hooked it and crossed over to the wall rack containing phone books in their metal covers. If someone dropped down from another planet tomorrow, he'd get the idea that telephone directories, banks' ballpoint pens, and hotels' coat hangers are the most valuable commodities on earth, the way we nail them down.

I swiveled the Omaha white and Yellow Pages into reading position and looked up United States Government. The local Treasury office was in the federal building downtown, on South Fifteenth Street.

*   *   *

Bill Jurgenson looked like your next-door neighbor. He had curly black hair salted with gray, pale green eyes, and a wide, nondescript face that was showing a blue five o'clock shadow about two hours early. He wore brown oxfords, tan slacks, white shirt, and a blue rep tie shot with tan and red. His shirt sleeves were turned back a couple of rolls and his horn-rimmed glasses lay on the desk blotter in front of him. I put him at fifty-five, give or take. He looked more like a high-school principal than a G-man.

The desk wasn't Jurgenson's; it belonged to someone named K. Schotten, who was high enough up the bureaucratic ladder to rate a private office and not be expected to be in it. So we were.

With us was a young black man in a gray summer-weight suit. He was very tall and fit looking—a former Creighton Bluejay basketballer, I imagined—with an attentive, studious air about him. He had a vinyl-covered legal pad open and propped on his crossed knees. Bill Jurgenson had introduced him only as "Agent Robinson."

Jurgenson said, "I'm a little surprised to see you here, Mr., uh, Nebraska."

I'm used to that little, uh, pause before my name, as if the speaker isn't quite sure he's got it, uh, right.

"Me too. But my spies tell me you've been asking around about me. I figured I could do a better job than anyone else of satisfying your curiosity."

He considered that, and me, for a long moment. Then: "All right. The top question is, What are you doing fooling around in the Longo investigation?"

I told him. I wasn't sure that "fooling around" would have been my choice of words, but I told him. The whole truth and nothing but, as they used to say on *The Defenders*. I know this kind of attitude won't get me elected to the Private Eye Hall of Fame—whenever we're dealing with Officialdom we're supposed to haul out the big chip that comes in our membership kit, balance it on our shoulder, and talk extra tough—but if you're more interested in doing

your job than cracking wise, you fast discover that the boys
and girls with the badges are a lot more helpful if you don't
antagonize them *too* much.

Jurgenson listened attentively, glancing occasionally at
Robinson, who might have been a cigar-store Indian for all
the expression he displayed. When I finished, Jurgenson
picked up his glasses from the desk blotter and swung them
absently between the thumb and forefinger of his right hand.
"I think you've been up-front with me," he said. "I appreciate that, and I'm going to return the favor. We are dead-
ended. The file remains open, of course. But just between
us girls, we've moved on to other things. Us and the Bureau.
We've *had* to."

"What about the money? Has any more of it shown up?"

He swung the glasses some more. "Not dime one, except
for the fifty-dollar note Longo was carrying. We've circulated
the serial numbers, of course, and asked the banks to keep
an eye open for us, but it's a needle-and-haystack operation.
We're talking a lot of bills, in denominations from ones on
up. Even a small bank can't cross-check the serial number
of every single note that comes through. Fifties and hundreds
is about all we can hope for, and even then it's spot-checking,
is all. You can't blame 'em. They've got other business to
handle too."

"If none of the money's turned up, it means one of two
things," I said. "Either the robber is clever, laying low,
not spending the loot, biding his time. Or he's already vanished to parts unknown and the money just hasn't shown
up in the federal-reserve pipeline yet."

"*Three* things." This from Robinson. "He's getting the
money laundered. It would lower his profit margin: The
going rate locally is ten or twelve percent, higher if you
need to move a lot of hot money fast. But it would increase
his safety margin."

"Four," Jurgenson corrected. Robinson and I looked at
him. It was getting to be like a tennis match. "Longo stole

the money, Longo hid the money, Longo can't tell us where
the money is on account of Longo got himself iced."

I said, "Accomplices?"

"Doubtful. He had two pals, coupla lowlifes . . ."

"Abel and Patavena," I supplied.

"Yeah, whatever. OPD put them through their paces,
and we kept a close watch on them for a week or better.
Nothing. Personally, I think they're too stupid to play it
cool with money. They're the kind to go from welfare to
Ferraris overnight—you know: sub-tle."

"Not only that," I said. "I wasted my breath trying to
talk with them yesterday, and they let it slip that Longo
had a girlfriend on the side—"

Jurgenson turned to Robinson. "We got anything on that?"

Robinson was already paging through the gray folder that
had been balanced on his knees. "I don't think so, Bill."

"I sort of planted the notion that Longo, if guilty, may
have parked the dough with her, and they went after her
like greyhounds after one of those electric rabbits. They've
got money like they've got brains."

Jurgenson grinned. "Then we can forget about them. What
about this girl?"

"Eloise Slater." I gave him a twenty-five-words-or-less
rundown. "Sort of a cool customer. Like most of the people
who knew Gregg Longo, she doesn't faint dead away at
the speculation that he *might* have been crooked. Her position
is, if he was, he did a good job of keeping it from her."

"Huh." He was still dinking with the eyewear. On every
backswing, the lenses caught the afternoon sunlight that
angled through K. Schotten's Levolor blinds and flung it
against my sport shirt.

"What about taking it from the other direction," Robinson
put in. "Can she alibi Longo? Even for one or two of the
robberies?"

"She says not. They held their little get-togethers as time
and circumstance and desire dictated. I gather there was

no pattern, no set rendezvous; she says she doesn't know from dates."

"Huh," Jurgenson repeated. He stopped playing with the glasses and slipped them on.

"I already gave all this to the local cops," I said. "It might be worth having someone pay a call on Ms. Slater. Not that you need me to tell you how to do your jobs."

Jurgenson's mouth formed a humorless grin. "I always say, I'll listen to all the advice I can get—not that I'll *take* any of it. But you're right, we'll want to talk with this Slater woman, if only so we can say we covered the bases." He spoke the last sentence to Robinson, who nodded, making notes on the cover of the file, then turned back to me. "Thanks."

"No charge. Listen, maybe you could do me a little favor."

"Here it comes," Jurgenson said, grinning wider.

"I know you've got an investigation and all, but maybe you could go a little easy on Carolyn Longo. She's been through hell."

"We know that. And believe me, we've tiptoed as much as we could. We had to search her house. We had to question her, her neighbors—hell, you know the drill."

"Sure," I said, watching him closely. Bill Jurgenson was an okay guy, I felt, but I had no doubt that a successful conclusion to this case would amount to one very large feather in his cap . . . and that the opposite conclusion would likewise trigger the opposite result. Under such circumstances, anyone might get overeager. "But you know how it is with civilians," I said. "Just tread softly if you can. Like you have been," I added smoothly.

Jurgenson smiled at me just as smoothly. "You bet," he said.

CHAPTER
EIGHT

Wasting time in downtown Omaha is easier than it used to be, even just four or five years ago. Back then, the retail stores, the movie houses, even the restaurants were retrenching at the malls or drying up entirely. What was left wasn't much to get excited about . . . and you did *not* want to hang around too long past sundown. The Big O was treading a path well-worn by dozens of other American cities in the past quarter century: Its downtown district was fast becoming a business district, gray, faceless buildings full of gray, faceless people performing gray, faceless functions.

An effort was being made to reverse that. An expensive "face-lift" for the downtown riverfront. A pedestrian mall. New retail space—old space made new, rather—and the economic incentives necessary to lure merchants back. It was much too soon to tell whether the effort would pay off in the long run, and anyone who thought downtown Omaha would ever again be what it was thirty years ago was dreaming, but it was a step in the right direction. Sometimes the attempt is worth as much as the result. Sometimes it's worth more.

I bummed around the new and the novel, the strange, the bizarre, the unexpected, made a visitation to the central library, where I looked up my name in *Books in Print,* and was at my post in the yellow zone in front of the Omaha Olympic Club by the time the office buildings started hemorrhaging workers at four fifty-eight.

Young Desotel was a bit late this evening. I figured being in charge of food and drink for a posh, exclusive club must not be too bad a job. Regular hours, at least. Eight to twelve, one to five, Monday through Friday. Some poor flunky of an assistant manager probably got stuck with noons, nights, and weekends. Still, rank entails responsibilities as well as privilege: Tonight, for instance, Loverboy was required to burn the midnight oil. Oh, all right, the five twenty-seven oil.

I tagged him to his car park, then fell in behind and one lane over from his blue Toyota as we followed our time-honored route home.

Only we didn't.

Desotel left Dodge Street at the light at Park. I barely made it through on the pink without getting creamed by a VW bus that had obviously done its share of creaming in the last fifteen years. He doubled back onto Harney and, at Twenty-sixth, pulled into the lot of the Antenna Lounge— aptly named, since it sits virtually under Channel 7's broadcasting tower.

I went by, slowly, making sure Loverboy left his car and headed into the building. Then I circled the block and parked my car next to his in the lot.

Unusual. I'd been on the guy's tail for about a week, and this was the first time he'd deviated from the routine. Which either meant something . . . or didn't. Maybe he had finally lined up a hot date. Or maybe he just decided to stop for a cool one after a long day.

Not an entirely depressing thought. I was feeling a little parched myself.

I reached under the front seat and hauled out the little Vivitar 110 LF tele camera I'd been hauling around ever since I'd taken the guardian-angel job. The camera was small and discreet, it slipped easily into my shirt pocket, it shifted from normal fixed-focus snapshottery to "telephoto" at the push of a button, and it had a built-in electronic flash. It took a 110 film cassette that didn't produce pictures as crisp as thirty-five-millimeter film but was much easier and faster to load—and *un*load, if need be.

Best of all, it had set me back only eighteen bucks.

I locked up the glove compartment with the gun inside and left the door unlocked. The situation was not such that I anticipated needing firepower, but, with luck, it *would* be such that I would need to make a hasty getaway after taking a snap of Desotel and friend in intimate embrace.

Hey, I can dream, can't I?

The bar was filled nicely with escaped wage slaves. I spotted Desotel, alone, in a booth against the wall, and bellied up to the bar, as the poet has it. There was no reason to be coy or furtive: Loverboy didn't know me from Adam, or Adam Ant, or even Atom Ant. I could have sat right across from him, except that booth was taken. Secure in my anonymity, I treated myself to a beer and waited for developments.

I was better at waiting than Desotel was. He checked the gold watch on his wrist several times a minute, strummed a nervous tattoo on the table, shredded the cocktail napkin that had come with his drink, and cast anxious eyes toward the door every time it opened, which was frequently.

By the way, when I say "anxious," I *mean* anxious, with anxiety—not "eager."

About half a beer passed before Desotel's date arrived. I was disappointed. I'd sort of had my heart set on one of those statuesque, all-American blondes with a store-bought tan and perfectly capped teeth. But Loverboy's date was a man, a trim, lightly colored black man in a black suit with the barest of salmon pin-striping. He *could* have been the man I had seen Desotel with downtown.

Well, I said to myself, keep a good thought; Maybe Desotel was having an illicit tryst with the black fellow. These *are* the eighties, after all.

The black man seemed familiar, and a quarter of a second later I realized why: I'd seen him with Eloise Slater, or vice versa, that morning.

If coincidences didn't occur, we wouldn't have a word for them. But this coincidence put a decided strain on credulity. Which means I doubted the coincidence-ness of it.

The black man spotted Desotel, sat opposite him, ordered a drink, drank it. Desotel drank his drink. I drank my drink. Everybody drank his drink: It was a bar. The two men talked for nearly an hour. They had second rounds; I didn't. If there's one thing you learn in the P.I. dodge it's how to make a drink last. Desotel visited the head once; his companion, twice. I, having nerves and other vital components of steel, stayed put.

As was the case at the HoJo coffee shop, the bar was too noisy, the conversationalists were too quiet, and I was too far away to pick up any juicy details of their discussion—again, just snatches.

Desotel. I was beginning to think you weren't coming.
Friend. (unintelligible) . . . business.
Later on—
Friend. (unintelligible) . . . fast now.
Desotel (nibbling a fingernail). I don't know . . .
Friend. Better figure it out . . . (unintelligible).
Still later—
Friend. (unintelligible) . . . lot of money, man.
Desotel. I know that.

If I were the guess-hazarding type, I would have hazarded the guess, by the look of it, that the black guy was trying to sell the white guy a lot of whole-life insurance that white guy didn't think he wanted to buy. Good move: whole life's a racket. However, since the black guy didn't have the requisite brochures, loose-leaf binders, pie charts, free pens, and

other insurance-salesman impedimentia—or *any* impedimentia, for that matter—I didn't hazard that guess. Or any other.
The black man was trying to convince Desotel of something,
and Desotel wasn't too sure, and that's about as far as I
could take it.

But what about Eloise Slater? Where did she fit into the
picture? What possible connection could there be between
her and Loverboy? And how did the black man happen to
be the fulcrum?

Finally, the two men stood. I waited until they were out
the door, then hustled out after them.

They were standing in the lot near the other fellow's
car, the gray Eurosport, talking. The sky was a purplish
stain and the air was still, thick with moisture. I slid behind
the wheel of my car, started the engine, waited.

Eventually, the two concluded their remarks. The friend
unlocked the Eurosport. Desotel got into his Toyota.

I had intended the swift completion of my appointed
rounds, viz. follow Loverboy home and sit on him for an
hour or two, but as I sat and mulled over the incredible
coincidence of running into the black man twice in one
day—in the course of two otherwise unrelated investigations—I decided to leave Desotel alone and tag the Chevy.

Up behind Memorial Park, off of Western Avenue, the
Eurosport pulled into a narrow driveway in front of a trim,
brick-fronted house perched on a green bump of land above
the street. The garage was a tuck-under, and its door was
slowly rolling upward as the car entered the driveway. Desotel's friend wheeled right in like he owned the joint, which
meant he probably did, and the door slid down after him.

Mail delivery was to the door in that neighborhood, so
to check the box for a name would have been slightly unsub-
tle. I copied down the address, which appeared in brass
numerals over the garage door, and doubled back to Decatur
Street.

Decatur Street, where the answering machine fairly bulged

with telephone messages. Most of them were nothing, several were hanger-uppers, one was a writing assignment, albeit a small one: two-hundred words—slightly less than one double-spaced typewritten page—about the health hazards of extended-wear contact lenses, for the "Health Update" section in *Omaha Now!* magazine. They were willing to pay peanuts and, of course, they wanted it yesterday.

One call was from Carolyn, and it reminded me that I had to think of a good way to tell her about her husband and Eloise Slater, if there were a good way. I was even less enthusiastic about that assignment than the extended-wear contacts thing.

A third call was from a fellow named Cook or Kuck or something, telling me that he was with Callinan Development Corporation and that Mr. Timothy Callinan himself would appreciate hearing from me at my "earliest convenience."

Mr. Timothy Callinan was better known to most Omahans as Irish Tim. Why this should be has always been a puzzle to me, since Irish Tim was neither Irish nor was his name Tim. Irish Tim's name, as far as his parents were concerned, was Gabriel Solomon Rabinovitz, accent on the *o*, and not too many of our Rabinovitzes hail from the Old Sod.

Tim, no doubt, had good reason for changing name and nationality. Good to him, at least. Back fifty, fifty-five, sixty years ago, when Irish Tim began plying the first of his many trades, Omaha was a city sharply divided along numerous lines—race, religion, nationality, neighborhood. In large measure it still is today, but in those days the dividing lines were almost physical, and their strictures nearly impossible to surmount. At a tender age, young Gabe Rabinovitz, newly arrived to the profession of importing Canadian liquor in the last days of Prohibition, may have concluded that being Irish was a good career move.

Whatever his reasons, Irish Tim at least looked the part. He was a big man—not tall, but big—with a wide, solid belly and a head of wavy red hair that refused to go gray even after what must have been sixty-five, perhaps even seventy years.

In those years, Irish Tim Callinan had been in and out of more crooked, slightly crooked, and, yes, not-at-all-crooked schemes than even a television writer has ever thought of. Booze, gambling, rackets, you name it. Currently his main interest was real estate—legit, I was told, or as legit as that particular racket gets. And why not? Why risk your neck when there are semilegal ways of stealing money? Irish Tim and I had crossed paths but never swords now and then over the millennia, but I couldn't imagine what he wanted with me now.

There was a good way to find out.

It was past seven, but I took a chance and dialed up the corporate offices at the number that had been left on my machine. The phone rang twice, then I got a metallic *choonk!* in my left ear, followed by another ring, softer than the first two. The line had automatically switched over to an answering service.

"Seventy-six hundred," the operator answered in a tinny rush of words, omitting the exchange prefix.

"For Timothy Callinan."

"Yessir."

"Returning his call. My name is Nebraska. Like the football team—"

"Just a moment, please." A pause, the line still open. Then: "I have a message for you, Mr., uh, Nebraska. Mr. Callinan invites you to call on him at home this evening. Any time this evening."

"Thank you," I said, but I said it to a dead line.

There was no point in my asking where Callinan lived, and no point in her volunteering it. Everyone in Omaha knew that Callinan Development had built Emerald Place— Emerald, Ireland, Emerald Isle, Irish Tim, are you getting it?—as an excuse to give Tim a bird's-eye view of the city.

Emerald Place is an exclusive residential, office, and retail complex set back from Center Street out on the extreme west end of town. At the center of Emerald Place is a fifteen-story residential tower, and at the top of the tower sits Irish Tim. His digs, Callinan Development Corporation, and his Shamrock Realty Company between them conspire to eat up the available penthouse space. The twelve floors below that are residential. The bottom two floors are given over to numerous offices, three restaurants, a radio station, and too many of the type of retail operations that look askance at even a Gold Card.

Ringing Emerald Tower, as it was known, are town-house condominiums and smaller office-parklike workplaces, all interlinked by wide, meandering drives with names like Donegal, Ulster, and Londonderry.

No Shillelagh Avenue, I'm afraid.

Emerald Place may sound like a planned community, and as I navigated its loping, seemingly aimless streets, trying to get to the tower, it looked like one. It isn't. It's just a tony address that caters to those who believe "exclusive" is as good as something can get. Most of the people who work there don't live there. Most of the people who live there don't work there—don't work anywhere much at all at very much of anything. The place is by no means self-sufficient. Its denizens are as much a part of the city as the vagrants sleeping in cardboard boxes down along the Missouri River, although such notions tend to give the upper crust upset tum-tums.

It occurred to me that a great many of the residents probably whiled away the long hours over dinner and drinks at the Omaha Olympic Club. Circles within circles.

Weeks passed. By keeping it ever to my left, I eventually came to the tower. Wasn't there something like this in *The Lord of the Rings?*

Emerald Tower featured 'round-the-clock valet parking, of course—I'd've been disappointed at anything less—but

I skipped it and planted the car myself in a surface lot separated from the building by a long curved drive. I don't like other people driving my car.

The lot was full of Mercedeses and Volvos, Audis and Saabs and BMWs. I spotted a DMC, a couple of Porsches, even a Tojan. The Tojan is a luxury sports car manufactured by an Omaha-based company, Knudsen Automotives. They say they came up with the name "Tojan" by dropping the *r* out of "Trojan." It adds up all right, but it doesn't explain why anyone would want to name a thirty-thousand-dollar car after a condom.

I tucked the old Impala between a cute little Mercedes two-seater convertible and one of the new, sleek T-bird Turbos.

"See if you can pick up some good habits," I told my car as I buttoned it up.

The doorman or concierge or whatever he was supposed to be cornered me in a foyer as big as my living room, pronounced my name into a gold-plated French-telephone receiver—no "uh" between "Mr." and "Nebraska": this *was* a class operation—pronounced me clean, and depressed a button on the space-age console of his desk. Double smoked-glass doors swung outward and admitted me to the holy of holies.

Okay, so it was just the lobby. It was an expensively done up lobby, replete with overstuffed, over-modern furniture, exuding all the warmth and charm of a dentist's office. Someone who had an uncle in the mirror-tile business had handled the paneling: diagonal strips, two-inch-wide oak alternating with two-inch-wide strips of dark reflective glass. Oak-mirror-oak-mirror-oak-mirror—now I knew how a strobe light must feel. I entered the nearest of three elevators, the one the doorman had pointed out. It shot me to the fifteenth floor in about the same amount of time it took you to read those words.

And it opened on Irish Tim's world.

The first thing I noticed was the carpet, wall-to-wall, very plush—and green. Real green. "I'll Take You Home Again, Kathleen" green. It looked like the Old Sod itself. And it looked overdue for a mowing.

The second thing I noticed was the woman. She had bright red hair piled high on her head and cascading down the back of her neck. She wore a shimmery black floor-length number, gathered at the throat and exposing the silky, unblemished whiteness of her arms and back. Her eyes were wide and green—not the gaudy green of the carpet but the deep and lustrous green of emeralds. Her features were regular, her chin maybe just a shade too prominent.

"Mr. Nebraska? I'm Maureen. I'm the housekeeper. Mr. Callinan is in the den, if you'd care to walk this way . . ."

I'd have walked any way she said, but I have far too much class to have said so.

The living room gave way to a formal dining room, off of which was a short, wide hallway leading to the den and, presumably, the apartment's bedrooms. The green carpet followed us the whole way.

Maureen tapped at the door of the den and opened it.

The room was dark, or nearly so. Illumination was in the form of a three-headed track-light rig that threw incandescent beams against the ceiling in a corner near the door. That, and the soft electronic glow from a twenty-five-inch color television monitor in the far corner of the room.

The den was a real den, not a spare bedroom pressed into service. It was a split-level affair. The door opened to the work space, where an ornate antique desk was positioned in the indirect light from the ceiling rig, and two straight chairs, also antique, or good reproductions, sat opposite the desk as if waiting for something. On the other side of the door was a round table, not antique, ringed with half a dozen comfortable-looking molded-plastic chairs. On the wall over the table was a write-on, wipe-off board. Over the desk was a framed antique map showing the counties of Ireland.

Eight feet from the door, the floor dropped a step to the playroom. A low leather couch sat against the long wall to the right; opposite, against the left wall, stood a wall unit loaded with stereo equipment, records, tapes, and compact discs, books, magazines, and general bric-a-brac. In the leftmost corner stood the television—stereo, of course—with a built-in VCR and a satellite-dish tuner resting atop it.

The back wall was glass, floor to ceiling. The city was growing gray beyond the panes, scarlet slashes tinging the sky, snaking away from the long sunset taking place on the other side of the building. Here and there across the city, lights glowed and blinked against the coming night.

In a leather recliner near the sofa sat Irish Tim.

"Thank you, Maureen," he said in a brogue so thick you couldn't cut it with a knife and fork. "We'll be havin' a drop in here, if y'd be so kind."

Maureen affected a kind of curtsy and departed, closing the door. When she had, Callinan said, "So, then, you received me message."

"Hello, Irish."

He picked up a long, thin, rectangular box. A track-light unit over the couch came to life. The television went black. "Would you be wantin' somethin' to eat?" His voice was a rough, pleasantly raspy tenor. "Me, I finished up a while ago—a man of regular hours, I'm afeared—but Maureen'd be glad to put somethin' together . . ."

I dismissed it with a gesture. "Although if the food is on a par with the surroundings, and especially the help . . ."

Tim chuckled modestly and made a self-deprecating movement of one meaty hand.

"By the way," I said, seating myself on the couch he indicated with another gesture, "we're all pals here, so how's about we drop the Barry Fitzgerald impressions? You're about as Irish as I am, Gabe, which isn't very."

His big face darkened for an instant, and anger flashed in his eyes like heat lightning. But it only lasted an instant.

The darkness passed and a hissing sort of laugh exploded from him. "Well, then," he said, and with only the barest trace of anything that could be called a brogue. "I've been talkin'—talk*ing*—that way so long, it's like second nature to me." He laughed again, and it was calmer, less sputtery. "Nothing worse than a convert, eh? Religion, politics, nationality, temperance—doesn't matter: He always takes it too far."

I knew what he meant. A nonsmoker who shook the habit is ten times more opposed to the weed than someone who never smoked. Fifty years ago, or more, Gabriel Solomon Rabinovitz had adopted the stereotypical Irish caricature as protective armor. He didn't need it anymore, but it was by now, as he himself said, second nature. Maybe even first: How long do you have to affect something before it's no longer an affectation?

Tim inspected me a moment, a grin on his pleasantly ugly face. "I'd been thinkin'—" He paused, closed his eyes briefly in a heaven-help-us way, and started again, broguelessly: "I thought you were out of the private-eye game, Nebraska."

"A game, is it? I thought games were supposed to be fun." Another tap on the door, and Maureen entered bearing a teak tray. The tray held Waterford glasses, cocktail napkins, an ice bucket, an open bottle of Jack Daniel's and a new bottle of Jameson's. She placed the tray on a coffee table in front of the couch and knelt near me on the green carpet.

She lifted a glass, looked up at me, and said, "Ice?"

I was aware of a warm, vaguely spicy scent from her. "No."

Maureen broke the seal on the bottle and neatly filled a glass to the halfway point. She handed it and a small blue napkin to me, then put cubes in the second glass, poured the Daniel's over them, and took it to Irish Tim. Repeating the curtsy, a quick bent-knee thing, she left.

"I don't believe it," I said when the door had closed. "All this Old-Sod nonsense and you're drinking"—I lifted the square bottle—" 'Jack Daniel's Old No. 7 Quality Tennessee Sour Mash Whiskey'? I'm very disappointed, Tim."

He smiled at me over the rim of his glass, and the brogue was comically thick when he said, "Aye, well, there's no raison t'be tellin' anyone"—the brogue vanished—"that I never *could* stand that crap. To your health."

I'll drink to that, and did.

The whiskey was hot going down. Then it hit my stomach and started a low, soothing glow that seemed to spread out from my belly in smooth, warm fingers. I held the crystal to the light and inspected the contents. "The oldest of whiskies," I said.

"That's one thing it has going for it," Callinan agreed. "The Irish had whiskey eight hundred years ago. At least."

"*Uisge beatha*, or however you pronounce it. From *uisge* comes 'whiskey.' " I caught Irish Tim's glance. "One of the dubious side benefits of the writing life is you learn all sorts of wonderfully useless stuff. I did an article on spirits, oh, almost a year ago. Picked up all kinds of junk. *Uisge beatha*, for instance, or the fact that the Americans and Irish spell 'whiskey' with an *e-y* while everyone else—the Scots, the Welsh, the Canadians, the Japanese, the Aussies—drop the *e*. I'm murder at Trivial Pursuit."

Tim chuckled, a rich, full-bodied chuckle that seemed to begin somewhere down in the middle of his ample self, bubble up his windpipe, and escape through the small gap between his lips. He held his glass, nestled against his belly, between both of his large, blunt hands.

"Then you *are* still writing. I was confused—I'd been thinkin' somehow that you were out the detective game for good." If he realized he had slipped back into an Irish cadence, if not exactly a brogue, he gave no sign of it. "I been hearin' about this book of yours . . ."

"Unfortunately, more people have been hearing about it than have been buying it." I dragged out and put on the old wide-eyed innocent face. "Have you got yours yet?"

Irish Tim smoothed the red hair over his left ear. He

looked like he was afraid I might have a copy in my back pocket and expect him to hand over ten ninety-five for it if he admitted he hadn't bought it. You get used to that look in a hurry.

"Eh . . . no," he admitted. "Is it out already? Where'd a fella get a copy?"

You get used to that question, too. "Gee, I dunno," I said blandly. "Let's see . . . it's a book . . . how 'bout—a bookstore!"

He pursed his lips and gave me a look that was half-amused, half-relieved at not being put on the spot. "I'm takin' it, then, that you're not completely out of the business."

"It's sort of like a bad marriage: You're never really *out* of it. Why?"

"Well, because I hear around town, that you're lookin' into Mr. Gregg Longo's, ah, unexpected demise."

"News travels fast." The cops, the bartenders, the guy at Job Service, the construction foreman, Lou Boyer, any of half a dozen big-eared workers on Hascall Street or at Westroads—Irish Tim could've learned of my interest in Longo's death from any of them. I knew better than to ask his source, or knock myself out trying to guess.

"That it does," Callinan agreed. "Are you?"

It was a rhetorical question. Irish Tim was plugged in well enough to find out what color underwear I had on if he really wanted to know. I nodded.

"I wonder why."

"That's an easy one: I'm being paid to. You knew Longo?"

"We had some business. I suppose the grievin' widow wants you to clear her poor dead husband's good name."

"Do you?" I took a sip of my drink—a small one. I'd had no dinner, and I didn't want the liquor sneaking up on me. "It's funny, I can't help wondering what your interest is, Irish."

He paused for a sip of his drink. Light touched a walnut-

sized stone set in a gold ring on his right hand and scattered
in ten different directions. "As I mentioned, poor Mr. Longo
and I had a business arrangement. A financial arrangement."

I sighed. "How much was he into you for, Tim?"

"Ten."

"And the vig?"

His pale eyes scanned the room lazily. "Oh . . . about
the same."

"Good Jesus," I said softly. "Ten grand out at one hundred
percent interest. Nice work if you can get it. Ponies?"

"Ponies, ball games, prizefights, state lotteries. Mr. Longo
was the sort who'd be willin' to put money on whether a
rabbit could get across a highway without bein' flattened
by a truck."

I wagged my head in disbelief—mild disbelief. Lou Boyer
had said that Longo enjoyed an occasional bet, as I think
he put had it. Ten grand's worth indicated a hell of a lot
of occasions, but Boyer may not have known. Compulsive
gamblers are like alcoholics in a lot of ways, and one of
the ways is they get very good at hiding their illness. Boyer
had also said that Longo never got past thinking that the
riches of Croesus were about to land in his lap. It looked
like he had taken some steps, some big steps, to try to
make it happen. Had he then had to take even bigger steps
to bail himself out of trouble with his banker?

I said, "What's the due date?"

"Oh, well, it had already come and gone by the time
Mr. Longo died."

"Tch," I said, or something much like it. "And you can't
exactly make a claim for recovery on his estate."

"No, not *exactly* . . . but after a fashion, perhaps. Y'see,
if people are right in thinkin' Mr. Longo was responsible
for those banks bein' robbed, well, then, there's—what do
they say—seventy-five or eighty thousand dollars unaccounted for somewhere."

"Seventy-eight seems to be the working figure." Although

the cops had not released the exact number, Irish Tim would know it. And Tim forgetting a dollar amount was only slightly more likely than you forgetting your middle name.

"Do tell. It seems to me that with a bright, talented lad like yourself makin' inquiries, well, that seventy-eight thousand might just get itself found. You see what it is I'm gettin' at?"

"Yes, believe it or not, I do."

He looked across the room at the stereo gear and frowned at it. "Now, let's understand each other. I only want my due. Twenty thousand. Twenty, and not a penny more. And I'll pay you a finder's fee—say, ten percent? Fifteen?— out of that twenty."

"What about the remainder?"

The big man shrugged. "No concern of mine, surely. I'm only interested in my due."

"But why should I give any of it to you? Assuming there's any to be found, I mean, and that I find it. If I'm honest, I turn it all in. If I'm not, I pocket the whole bundle of joy and not merely, what, two thousand?"

Irish Tim smiled. "Say three. I like you." He shifted in his chair and leaned forward, narrowing the four-foot gap between us. "Nebraska, I've been around a long time and I've been a lot of things but mostly what I've been is a gambler. D'you see? Everything I've ever done's been a gamble. Now I'm gamblin' on you to be like most people— neither too honest nor too dishonest. I'm thinkin' you wouldn't mind turnin' a dollar or two for yourself if the greater portion of the money would be gettin' to where it's supposed to go. That's what honesty is, y'know, a matter of degrees. I mean, the man owed me twenty thousand and I'm only tryin' to recover it. I could've told you he owed me fifty, sixty, seventy. I didn't. Why?"

"You knew I wouldn't buy it."

He pretended to look offended. "Because I'm basically an honest man."

"Lending money out at a hundred percent interest isn't honest, Timmy. It's usury, and it's slightly illegal."

He waved it aside as if it were an annoying insect. "You're talkin' law. I'm talkin' *honest*. If a man's willin' to borrow from another man at a particular rate, what's that to anybody but the borrower and the lender? . . . Anyhow, I didn't want to see you so we could hold a debate. I wanted to discuss my little business proposition with you. What d'you say?"

He emptied his glass, reached for his bottle, and nodded at the other bottle with a question stitched across his face. I shook my head and said, "If I owed you twenty thousand and I didn't feel like paying it, what would happen to me?"

Callinan pursed his lips and put an inch of liquor into the bottom of his glass. "If we didn't both know how Mr. Longo . . . expired, I might think you'd be hintin' that *I* had a hand in it." He tested the whiskey, found it as satisfactory as the first glass had been, and risked a larger swallow. "That's always been a problem, y'know, in the trade. What to do with a welsher. In the old days, you'd break an arm or a leg, or both, as a kind of warnin'. If the warnin' didn't happen to take . . ." He raised and lowered his shoulders.

"Well, they still go in for that, some of the boys. But the problem is, you still don't have your money. Me, I'll give a fella a good stern warnin', maybe two. And then I'll . . . repossess."

"Repossess? Repossess what?"

"Whatever. Car, furniture, clothes. Things I can resell, so as to not only teach the offendin' party a lesson but also recover at least some of my outlay." He sipped silently. "Much more civilized and practical, wouldn't you say?"

Maybe I would have, but I didn't. I said, "If Longo owed you twenty thou and had seventy-eight thou in a shoe box, a very *large* shoe box, why wouldn't he just pay you?"

"I've asked myself the very same. Could it be the lad

was plannin' to disappear with *my* money as well as the banks'?"

I looked at him. "Now that would be pointless. You're networked better than CBS. Longo could disappear anyplace he'd like and you or one of your friends would find him inside of six months. Longo knew that. He must have, or he'd've skipped long ago—skipped if he couldn't pay, pay if he could."

The red-haired man plucked at his lower lip. "You overestimate my influence," he said. "I won't tell you I don't have friends here and there, but . . ." He shrugged.

"If Longo was going to skip, he'd've skipped. If he had almost eighty grand, he'd've had plenty of money to do it in style, too. He also would've been able to pay you off and still have almost sixty thou to eke by on for a while. He didn't do either. Doesn't that suggest to you that perhaps Longo didn't have the money?"

Irish Tim spread his hands, his glass held lightly in his left hand, his right hand empty, large and meaty. "That bein' the job y've cut out for yer ownself," he said, the situation-comedy brogue fully back in place. "If the dearly departed was indeed innocent as the angels, then of course there'll be no money to recover. But if there should be . . ."

I rested the glass against my lower lip. "Yes," I said. "If there should be . . . What about his wife?"

"The grievin' widow? Carolyn?" It bothered me that he knew her name, although of course he would. "What about her? . . . Ah, no, I see. You're thinkin' I might like to take some of my losses out of her own no doubt delectable hide." He shook his big, homely head. "No, lad. You should know me better'n that. I've no quarrel with her."

I downed some whiskey. Its flavor and aroma were at once distinct and subtle. Now that I was used to it, I found its effect on my mouth and tongue to be less burning, more prickling—teasing. And it had a nice way of sort of softening the edges of the world, rather than blotting them out like

Old Fedora and the other industrial-grade brands of buck-fifty-a-gallon paint remover that I usually drink.

I said, "Either Longo robbed those banks or he didn't."

Tim said, "Those would appear to be the only possibilities."

"Let's say he did."

A crooked smile made its way across Irish Tim's oversized face. "All right, let's."

"And let's say that through diligence, superior intellect, and good luck, I trip over the loot."

"Which a smart young lad like your ownself is liable to do."

"And then let's say I decide to keep the money for myself."

Irish Tim Callinan's smile didn't budge. "You wouldn't do that. Not all of it. You're too honest, like most people."

"Okay, I'm honest. So let's say I find the money and I turn it all—*all*—over to Uncle."

He made a noise with his mouth, kind of like, *Tchah*, and said, "I said honest, not stupid."

"Sometimes they're the same thing."

The smile stayed put, but now it didn't reach as far as his eyes. "Then *I* would be very disappointed in *you*, lad," Tim said quietly in his gravelly tenor. "I'm thinkin' you're smarter than that."

Which I could take any way I liked.

Maureen waited at the end of the short corridor outside the den. Irish Tim must have somehow signaled her that I was leaving. I followed her through the dining room and on into the living room, admiring the ebb and flow of her hips under the shiny dress, the shock of red, red hair against her ivory back. She did not have the pink, slightly mottled skin of some redheads . . . yet I didn't doubt for an instant that the color of her hair was the work of Mother Nature, not Lady Clairol.

At the door, Maureen stopped, turned, and put a slim

hand on my arm. It was warm—her hand; my arm felt like ice beneath it.

Her eyes were impossibly green, her lips impossibly pink. They parted. "Mr. Nebraska . . . would you do something for me?"

She was probably accustomed to men answering that question with, "Anything." I managed, "If I can."

She left me, left the room, and was gone a full minute, perhaps longer.

If my life were a detective novel, she'd've returned as naked as the day she was born, her flaming hair down around her milky shoulders.

In the event, when she returned she was fully dressed as before. But now she carried something, a small object, in both hands. She crossed the room, smiling, and held it out to me.

It was a book. It was my book. It was The Book.

She said, "Will you autograph your novel for me?"

I sat behind the wheel of the car, listened to the radio, looked at Emerald Tower, and thought.

Shadows had lengthened and blackened while I was in the Enchanted Kingdom. The sun was making its last stand off behind the tower, and as the light died, so did the heat, a little. But the air lost none of its moisture. The evening was still, the air was stale with a kind of vague fishy smell to it.

The woman on the radio said the temperature had dropped from eighty-four to eighty-two in just an hour and made it sound like a big deal. Then she played "Runaway," by Del Shannon. The singer, not the mystery writer. Good song, but I like Elvis's "live" version better. It's got guts. Shannon whines; Presley growls.

By the way, there's no arty significance to that song. It's just what the station I happened to be tuned to happened to be playing when I happened to be listening.

I thought about Irish Tim Callinan. Actually, I thought about Maureen, although "thought" isn't the most accurate verb, and then after a while I made myself think about Irish Tim.

Callinan lied when he said he was a gambler. Maybe he had been, once upon a time, but no more. You don't reach Irish Tim's plateau—you don't get Emerald Towers and two or three legitimate front corporations and hot-and-cold-running Maureens—by being a gambler. You take risks, certainly. The very nature of Irish Tim's "business" was risk. But risk can be managed; out-and-out gambling never can, not from the gambler's side, which is how the Las Vegases and the Atlantic Citys pay for the lights.

All of which meant Callinan didn't just stick a pin in the phone book and hit my number.

He called me for a reason, and that reason was—what? He knew Longo was guilty and he wanted the money? Why bother with me? Tim had access to any of a dozen guys who could track down the loot, unencumbered by such excess baggage as the law, ethics, or even common courtesy.

But if Callinan knew for a fact that Longo *wasn't* guilty, he'd have even less reason to have me in for a drink.

Which meant Callinan didn't know for a fact either direction . . . but *did* know that Longo was smack in the middle of the picture no matter which way things fell.

And so was I.

No, Irish Tim wasn't gambling. He was hedging. If Longo didn't have the money, Tim was no worse off than before. But if Longo *did*, and I somehow managed to get my mitts on it, and Callinan had given me things to think long and hard about. . . .

Tim had indeed given me some things to think about. But not about him, and not about me.

About Gregg Longo.

CHAPTER
NINE

The guy behind the bar put a napkin, a glass, and a bottle of Falstaff in front of me, in that order. I moved some of the beer into the glass and, while the head went down, casually swiveled on my stool and inspected the Grain Bin.

Business was good. I don't suppose the owners were in much danger of exceeding legal occupancy, but trade was brisk. Most of the tables and all of the booths on the main level were spoken for. I had plenty of company at the bar, too. By the sound of it, the mezzanine was given over to a private party. In the back of the room, the pinball and video machines *ping*ed and *beep-beep*ed and *whoop-whoop-whoop*ed under the skilled hands of kids who looked like high schoolers to me but were probably college kids on summer vacation. The combined effects of several dozen conversations conducted simultaneously put the noise level at a steady but tolerable decibel reading, disrupted only occasionally by an excited impromptu cheer from the back room or raucous laughter from upstairs.

The clientele was a decidedly nontrendy mix—the college kids in their jeans and whatever kind of casual shoe was in that season; businessmen and salesmen who had stopped for a quick one after work and, accidentally or otherwise, lost track of the time; urban and not-so-urban cowboys and their paramours; and the less-easily classifiable—workers from the oil depot down the road, guys from the truck stop, passers-through who had wandered over from the Cloud 9 Motel with its Phone In Every Room.

I added enough beer to top off the glass, sipped, and scanned the room again for Eloise Slater.

The way hard-drinking, hardboiled detectives get to be so hard drinking, I figured, is by spending so much time hanging around bars. I seemed to be spending a fair amount of my free time in them myself these days. No way around it, though. When the people you're spooking around after hang around in bars, so do you.

Eventually I found Eloise Slater. More correctly, she found me. I had my eyes on the right side of the room when a voice in my left ear said, "I *thought* that was you."

I turned. She was wearing a grin and a hot-pink knit shirt tucked into tight black leather pants. Under the shirt, nothing. Under the pants, hard to say. The pointed toes of shiny, sapphire-blue high-heeled shoes showed under the pants' tapered legs. Her belt was a length of gold chain, drawn through the loops and secured with a small golden padlock. I smiled. "You thought right," I said.

She set a round cork-lined tray on the rubber mat between two upright chrome rails on the bar. "Two Bud Lights, two Coors, tonic twist," she told the bartender in a rapid monotone. He nodded at about the point where you or I would be saying *Wha-at?*, and went to work. Eloise Slater tucked a lock of dark hair behind her right ear, looked at me sidelong, and said, "I'm pissed off at you."

"I'm not surprised."

"You sicced the cops on me," she said quietly but forcefully, on the tail of a quick glance around to make sure no one was paying attention. No one was. "That was a crappy thing to do."

"Just doing my job. As they said at Nuremberg. Anyhow"—I examined her from the floor up—"you don't look much the worse for wear. What'd they do? Ask you a few questions, look around the house? Hell, after this morning's festivities, it must have been a cakewalk."

Despite herself, she laughed. "They didn't have to look around much: Everything's still piled up in the middle of the place. I had some errands to run today, and I really just didn't feel like dealing with the mess."

"Uh-huh." I drank some beer. "Well, I'm sorry I blew your cover, but so it goes. Look, I need to ask you a couple more questions."

"What about?"

"Longo. And things."

"Things, huh?" One slender eyebrow inched upward speculatively. "I'll bet."

The tray was reloaded now, the tab smartly anchored to the cork with water or whatever. She hoisted it onto her hip with easy, practiced skill and gave me a long, narrow look with her slitted dark eyes.

I watched her climb the wooden stairs to the mezzanine over the game machines.

I waited. It was a longish wait. That was all right. I dumped the rest of my beer into the glass and watched minuscule bubbles drift upward. Some of them clung to the inside of the glass. I wondered what determined which ones would stick and which ones would roll on up the glass and disappear into the quarter-inch of head floating on top.

Private detectives spend a lot of time alone, waiting, with nothing to do.

A few minutes later, Eloise was back with a trayful of empties, glasses as well as bottles. The bartender scooped up the glasses and dumped them into sudsy water under the counter. Then he grabbed the tray and, from three feet away, shot the bottles into a plastic-lined cardboard drum.

"Three Coors, three Falstaffs, Miller Lite, Coke," she told the bartender. To me: "Well?"

"Well?"

"Well, you said you had some questions. Ask. Or are you sure you just came here to talk?"

I watched the bartender work, quickly but not hurriedly, and said, "Aw, now you know." I swallowed some beer. "I came here to drink, too."

"Right," she said.

Again the tray was full. Again she left. Again I waited. After an interval, she returned with another set of orders for the bartender and another sidelong glance for me.

I said, "This conversation would take less time if we were doing it by mail. Is there a possibility you could spare five minutes, five *consecutive* minutes, to talk to me?"

"I'm off tomorrow night," she said. A strange half-smile snaked across her lips. "That'll give us all night."

"I just need five minutes."

She looked at me under drooped eyelids. "What the hell. Hey, Denny." The bartender looked up. "I gotta take five. Get Shelly to cover for me, will you."

"You don't go on break till nine."

"Screw you."

We stepped out onto the boardwalk fronting the place. The world was that funny blue-gray you get only on long summer evenings, only in the Midwest.

Between its own lamps and the illumination spilling back from the front of the old elevator, the parking lot was well lighted. Clouds of insects hung around the lights. A few kids hung around the cars. Two men and two women, the men in bowling shirts that had Kingpins across the backs, came up the walk. I waited until they passed us and entered the bar. Then I said, "This morning you said something about Longo once talking about ro—"

"You got a car here?" She smiled again, the strange half-sleepy, half-smirky smile. "I need to get off my feet a minute."

I said yeah and we went along to the far end of the building where the Impala was parked. She slumped on the seat on the passenger's side, propping her feet against the dash. She let out a long sigh, then, as an afterthought, asked if I minded.

"Please," I said magnanimously. "My dashboard is your dashboard. I've never been a cocktail waitress, but those don't strike me as ideal footwear for the endeavor."

She stabbed a heel into the dash and waggled her foot. "Eight hours on these can be a killer, but they help you get bigger tips."

I looked at her shirt.

"*Tips*," she said, "ti-*puhs*." She grinned. "But you've got the idea. I wear a shirt lets you get a little peek at my boobs, pants so tight I practically have to grease my legs to get into them, and heels that half the guys in the place would love to have me wear walking up and down their backs—you think they're gonna be noticing how long it took me to make their change?"

"Very scientific."

"Swinging your ass beats running it off."

"I think I came across that one in *Bartlett's* the other day."

Eloise gave me a long look. Then she leaned across, took my head in her hands, and held her mouth very close to mine. I could smell her breath, toothpaste and lipstick, smell her perfume floating over the fainter but pungent smell of cigarette smoke. Her lips were sweet and smooth and cool with gloss. They drifted lightly over mine, then harder, harsher. She ended the kiss, moved her face away. Then she ducked back in and bit my lower lip, lightly but definitely.

She pulled away. "You sure *that* isn't what you came for?" The laugh was a bark.

I said, "Maybe you could take a course at the YWCA or someplace, develop a little self-confidence."

She smirked. "You liked what you saw this morning, at my place, you liked the things I told you, the things I said

I'd do to you. *For* you. You know you did. But you're like
the guy who wants to buy a dirty magazine and's embarrassed,
so he gets *Time* and *Newsweek* and everything else to try
and cover it up."

"Actually, I get dirty magazines because I'm embarrassed
about buying *Time* and *Newsweek*. Listen. This morning you
said Longo had once mentioned the idea of robbing a bank."

Her laugh was even harsher than before. *"That's* the best
you can do? Jesus . . ." She shook her head, grinning.
Then she reached between her bent knees and opened the
glove compartment. "You got any cigarettes in here?"

"No." I reached under her legs and closed the little door.
"I quit six years ago."

"Yeah? I quit once for a whole week, but it didn't last.
How'd you do it?"

"Easy. I ran out of money and cigarettes at the same
time. And speaking of money . . ."

Eloise sighed elaborately. "Like I told you, like I told
the guys from the Treasury, it was just, like, *talk,* all right?
It didn't mean anything. It wasn't like Gregg was showing
me an outline of exactly how he planned to rob banks."

"How'd he happen to make the remark? What led up to
it?"

She shook her dark head, frowning. "I don't know. I
don't remember—that's how unimportant it was. I suppose
Gregg was talking about how tight things were, you know,
and then he said, like, 'What I ought to do is go rob a
bank.' Something just that stupid." She looked at me, the
frown still in place.

"Did Longo talk a lot about money?"

"Doesn't everyone?"

"I mean, was he preoccupied with it? Did he talk about
being in hock to someone in a big way?"

"He owed *everybody*. He owed on his house and his car
and most of the junk they bought, him and his wife, since
he went out of business . . ."

"Not that kind of stuff. This would be something he owed to one person."

"He owed *me* a hundred bucks."

This was getting nowhere.

I said, "Did he ever talk about needing to get hold of a lot of money, fast, in order to make a big payment?"

Lips pursed in concentration, she shook her head.

"Did he ever talk about leaving town?"

"Not really."

"What does 'not really' mean?"

She snorted in exasperation. "Jesus! It means he said it once or twice the same way he said he should rob a bank. He'd be real down about nothing turning up, like a job, I mean, and then he'd say how maybe him and me should just up and leave town, you know, see if things were better someplace else."

"Was there a time . . ." I paused, thinking how to phrase it. "Did there come a time when Longo didn't seem so concerned about money?"

"Like after one of the banks was knocked over?" Again with the half-smirk. "You asked it before. Look, why'n't you just tell me what you *really* want?"

What I really wanted was a peek inside of Longo's head, take a look at his attitudes, his feelings, and try to get a handle on whether or not the little weasel had actually robbed those banks. Was he consumed with worry about money and then, suddenly, not—as if his money trouble had simply evaporated? Lou Boyer told me that Longo had never grown out of thinking that his ship would come in sooner or later. Did Longo have reason to think it finally had? Had Longo planned to skip town with or without the money he owed Irish Tim Callinan? Or when his life bled out of him as he lay on the pavement that summer night, was his last thought that he had at least escaped the long arm of the loan shark?

Ever since I had connected a face with the name Gregg Longo, the other night with Carolyn—ever since I had seen the pictures of Longo on Carolyn's dresser and had compared the face in them to the face in the faded pictures I still carried in my head after twenty years—I had been mentally reviewing the only clear memory I had of him.

High school. Junior year, I think, but it could just as easily have been senior year. There was a room, a glorified boiler room, really, in the basement of the school building. The room was a litter of junk and janitor's supplies, a tangle of pipes and steel electrical conduit. Some of the teachers would sneak in there for a smoke between classes.

At some point during the year, several of the less academically inclined members of the student body conspired to flush every toilet in every bathroom in the building at exactly the same instant.

The escapade was planned with the exactitude of a surgical air strike. Sufficient numbers of troops, girls as well as boys, were drafted in order to ensure that every crapper in the joint was activated. Watches were synchronized—in some cases, no doubt, stolen and then synchronized—with fanatical precision. The operation went off on time. And the result was as you'd expect.

The waste pipes that ran across the boiler-room ceiling—ancient pipes, pipes that probably had been laid by the Romans—burst under the unaccustomed strain.

And eight thoroughly drenched high-school teachers evacuated the room, howling like fiends loosed from hell.

Only a few of the scapegrace organizers were ever bought to justice. One of them—he proudly claimed the stunt was his bright idea—was a zit-faced greaser named Gregg Longo.

That was *my* Gregg Longo, the single well-formed recollection I had of him. Hard to reconcile that with the picture of a calculating, gun-wielding holdup man who not only successfully robbed a series of banks for a total of not quite eighty thousand dollars, but also secreted the take so cleverly that now, coming up on a month after his death, it still remained hidden.

Who was Gregg Longo? A basically good man caught up in bad times, bad ideas, bad luck? An innocent lunk who happened to be in the wrong place at the wrong time? A modern Dillinger, crafty enough to have pulled off his jobs without anyone being the wiser? Which? Who was he? What had gone through his head as he died? Anger? Confusion? Relief? What?

I shared none of this with Eloise Slater. I doubted that she knew any of the answers. I doubted that she had considered any of the questions. Eloise Slater was not the sort of woman given to long musings about other people's attitudes, behavior, or comments. Her antennae were not sensitive enough to pick up on the nonverbal signals.

Correction: I had the distinct feeling that she was very good at receiving a particular *type* of nonverbal transmission, namely, the sexual variety. But nothing beyond that. Her relationship with Gregg Longo had been almost purely physical. She had volunteered as much when I interviewed her that morning. I would have been very surprised to discover that her concern, her sensitivity, extended beyond their little bondage-and-discipline sessions.

As if to confirm my suspicion, her hand went to my thigh. Her nails dug in through the thin summer-weight slacks I wore. Then her hand began to meander slowly, very slowly, up my leg.

I looked into her eyes and said, "Who's the black guy you met after I left you this morning?"

My leg might have been electrified, the way she jerked her hand away from it. "You fucker," she hissed, "you followed me!"

I caught her wrist as the nails came up toward my face, held it a moment, letting her push, letting her see it was futile. Her other arm, her left arm, moved, and I pinned it against the car seat with my right shoulder. Then, carefully and slowly, I forced her right arm back.

She held her breath as long as she could. Then it broke in a ragged gasp. "You bastard, cut it out!"

"What's the matter, Queenie, you don't like being on the receiving end?" I let go of her wrist.

"Fuck you," she said.

"Maybe some other time. Have your girl call my girl." The hand came up again; this time the palm was open. I brought my arm up and hers crashed into it, hard, which hurt her more than it hurt me.

"Ow, goddammit!" She massaged her inner forearm, midway between the wrist and the elbow. "Christ, you're a bastard."

"So you've already said. What about the guy this morning."

"I oughta sic the goddamn cops on *you*," she said petulantly.

"Be my guest. I know several who'll be happy to help you. And tell you that there's no law against following someone. I think it's illegal to follow fire engines and so on, but there isn—"

"Screw you. Why should I tell you anything?"

I shrugged elaborately. "You might as well. I followed your friend home this evening, I know where he lives, I can find out who he is. You'd just be saving me some time is all. Saving *you* some time, too, because if you *don't* tell me, I can pretty well guarantee that the boys with the badges are going to have some new questions for you come morning, and this time they won't be so easygoing."

"Fucker," she said, but silently, lips only. She eyed me warily for a long stretch, guardedly, gauging the seriousness of my threat, trying to decide how much of what to tell me, trying to decide what I would believe—hell, I don't know. These things don't go shooting across people's eyes like stock-market quotes.

Finally she puffed disgustedly, making a big deal of it. "Monroe James," she said sourly. "That's his name, Monroe James. He's just a friend of mine. Happy?"

"Tickled pink. I think it's funny you scampered off to meet this product of patriotic, if dyslexic, parents immediately after Abel and Patavena ripped your place apart looking for the Longo treasure."

"Who cares what you think," she said acidly. I let a little

time pass, let her mull things over. Again, she sighed and shook her head. "Look, Monroe's a friend, okay? An old friend. We get together from time to time."

"But not in the Dungeon of Pain."

She made a face at me. "A friend," she repeated. "*Just* a friend. Okay?"

"What did you meet him for this morning?"

"Nothing. Just to get together. You probably don't understand what I'm talking about, since you probably don't have any friends."

"You thanked him for meeting you. When you first arrived. I heard that—and some other parts of the conversation." A little bit of invention, that last part, but I didn't think it'd hurt to leave her wondering what else I might have overheard. "When old friends get together, they say things like, 'I'm sure glad we could get together.' Not 'Thanks for meeting me.' So?"

"So what? Look, I was upset. Wouldn't you be? These two creeps come busting in, first one, then the other, waving guns, carrying on about Gregg and me and money I don't have, ripping my place apart . . . then you and your twenty questions." Her voice changed—it softened, took on a low, quiet, sympathy-eliciting tenor. "I was upset. I needed a friend. So I called Monroe, and he was there for me."

"God love 'im. He wouldn't come over to your place?"

"I didn't want him to. I didn't want to be there. I didn't want to deal with it. I still don't. The place is still a wreck."

"So you said." I considered a fly working his way across the dashboard. The bluish parking-lot lights gave him a shadow as big as a terrier. "So you and Monroe James got together, you cried on his shoulder, he dried your tears and patted your tush and said there-there, and you went your separate ways."

She nodded, almost contritely.

"Where'd you go then?"

"Home."

"What'd you do?"

"I went to bed. I was bushed."

"Who's Jonathon Desotel?"

"I don't know."

I considered it.

"It's *true*."

"It probably is," I said. "Given a string of rapid-fire questions like that, a liar will try to hedge, stall, keep himself calm enough that he doesn't make any obvious slipups. Fast answers to fast questions tend to indicate truthfulness . . ."

"Well, all right."

". . . or that the respondent is an accomplished liar."

"Screw you," Eloise laughed and slapped my arm.

"What's James's story? What's he do for a living that he can pull away in the middle of the morning to hold hands with distraught friends?"

She ignored the sarcasm. "He's a financial consultant." I thought of Woody Allen's line: "I tell people what to do with their money until it's all gone." Maybe my whole-life crack hadn't been too far off the mark after all.

"Does he consult your financial?"

Eloise laughed. "*What* financial?"

"Well, you had a hundred to lend to Longo . . ."

"Which left me a balance of exactly ninety-two eleven in savings. You don't want to *know* about checking . . ."

She was right. I wanted to know about Monroe James and Jonathon Desotel. I wanted to know what business they had. Sure, James could have been advising Desotel about his finances, or trying to land Loverboy as a client, but it didn't feel right, didn't *smell* right. I've seen people on the business end of a high-powered salesman, I've been there myself and so have you, and Desotel's reaction just wasn't right. He was teetering on the brink, wanting to do something and *not* wanting to, or being afraid to, just as strongly. What? Where did Monroe James come in? Where did Eloise Slater come in? And what about Longo?

I became aware of Eloise's eyes on me. For something to say, I said, "Did your friend Monroe know your friend Longo?"

"I don't know. I don't think so. Why?"

"When was the last time you saw Longo?"

"Day before he got killed." Her hand was on my leg again. I don't know when it got there, while I was lost in thought, probably. The hand moved lightly, sinuously.

"What'd he talk about that day?"

"He didn't do much talking." Her hand moved up and her face moved closer. Her voice, already soft and low, softened further, melted into a bare whisper. "I didn't let him."

Closer. "I wouldn't let you talk much either," she whispered, harshly now. Her hand had moved up my leg about as far as it could. I seemed to be giving her the reaction she wanted. She smiled. "You talk too much," she said. "Think too much."

It wasn't a kiss. She bit again, hard: I tasted blood on my lower lip. At the same instant her hand moved, squeezed. She laughed when I drew back with a curse and pushed her away.

She popped open the car door on her side and jackknifed out. Then she leaned back in.

"Tomorrow night," she said. "*All* night."

Her laugh was canceled out by the slam of the door.

CHAPTER
TEN

Carolyn's street was a portrait of Middle America, summer, late twentieth century. Under the eerie glare of high-intensity streetlights, two kids played with a dog and a Frisbee. Across the street, the old couple out of *American Gothic* sat in plastic chairs on their concrete slab of a porch, taking a break from the heat inside. The old lady had one of those little battery-operated plastic fans. Next door, an obese man in striped walking shorts and a white undershirt that was hard-pressed to conceal his massive midriff fought with an oscillating sprinkler.

"Is there a water shortage?" I asked Carolyn when she opened her front door. I jerked a thumb at the neighbor. "That's usually why people water their lawns under cover of dark."

She rolled her eyes. "Mr. Pistelli has his own ideas about things. He says it's better to water at night and he doesn't believe you if you tell him it causes root rot. He also wears a black bowling shirt when he mows because he says black keeps you cooler."

"During the day?" She nodded. "He's wrong," I said.

"Don't tell me, tell him," she laughed.

We were in the living room by then. It was softly lighted by a torchière that threw its illumination against the high ceiling, to be scattered back from there. The day's newspaper was strewn across the sofa. So was the day's mail, consisting mainly of the dreaded window envelopes, from what I could see. In the corner, a nineteen-inch portable color television prattled away, ignorant of the fact that the audience had walked out on it.

Carolyn said, "I left a couple messages on your machine. I thought I'd hear from you today."

I looked at my wristwatch. "You thought right: It's still today."

"You always were the comedian."

"Union rules. Us hardboiled P.I. types gotta crack wise. Also gotta have the strength and smarts of a musk ox. Wanna see me bend a quarter with my biceps?"

"Some other time, maybe." She gathered the paper together, folded it into a rough approximation of its original state, and threw the wad into an armchair. "Let me get some of this junk out of the way," she said while she got some of the junk out of the way. She pulled together the envelopes and waved them at me. "Want a few of these?"

"Thanks, I've got my own collection at home."

"The cost of things never goes down, does it."

"I read where the only thing that hasn't gone up about a bazillion times since the end of World War Two is the per-word rate paid by mystery magazines. Of course, I read it in one of the umpty-eleven mystery-writers' newsletters I get, so consider the source."

Carolyn threw the bills on top of the newspaper, chuckling politely. "What can I get for you? A drink?" She killed the TV picture. "There're a coupla beers in the fridge."

"Actually, a cup of coffee would be good, if it's no trouble."

"No trouble. Instant okay?"

"On second thought, a beer sounds good."

I followed her into the kitchen. It was a big old-fashioned—
old-fashioned, nothing: *old*—square room. Copper molds
hung on the wall, cookware hung from a wrought-iron rack
that looked like it had been picked up at Torquemada's
going-out-of-business sale. The sink was heavy white porce-
lain, no cabinetry surrounding the pipes beneath it. In fact,
there was no cabinetry at all in the room—no counter, no
cupboards. The stuff that goes into modern kitchens' cupboards and drawers was stowed in a small pantry at the
back of the kitchen, next to the back door, and on long,
thick shelves over the sink and near the stove. The stove
and the refrigerator, at least, were modern.

Carolyn popped open the icebox, stuck her head in, and
came out with a can of three-two beer and a Cool Whip
tub filled with ice cubes. She put the tub on a square-topped
wooden table situated under the medieval torture rack and
handed me the beer. "Glass?"

I squeezed the can. "Feels like aluminum."

She shook her head, disappeared into the pantry, and
emerged with a bottle of J&B. On her way back to the
table, she snagged an old-fashioned glass from the shelf
over the sink.

I peeled open the can and watched her build her drink.
Three cubes, a healthy splash of Scotch, no water. She
took a quarter-inch of liquid off the top and replaced it
before capping the bottle. Then she pulled out one of the
ladder-back table chairs and sat. I dragged out a chair and
sat opposite her.

It felt right. The homey kitchen, the rickety wooden table,
sitting there, just sitting there like that, with Carolyn. It
felt very right. It felt like maybe I should have been doing
it every night for the past twenty years. Come home to a
real house and a real wife after working all day at a real
job. None of this apartment shit. None of this sometimes-
marriage shit. None of this chase-the-rainbow shit. Real life.
Middle-class Middle America. Kids and dogs and mortgages

and orthodontia, church on Sunday and Rotary on Thursdays . . .

It could have been like that. It wasn't, but it could have been. Life is a string of choices, most of which we make without even knowing. Carolyn made hers. I made mine. Maybe they were right and maybe they were wrong. The problem with decisions, most decisions, is you never really know. Not really. You don't get to find out until ten minutes after you're dead. And then you don't care.

Carolyn was as much enmeshed in her thoughts as I was in mine. I floated out of my reverie and became aware of her looking at me, studying me, her lips faintly pursed, her eyes slightly narrowed.

I said, "I'll give you a penny for 'em. 'Course, you'll have to take an IOU."

She smiled mirthlessly. "I think we're wasting our time, Ivan," she said. "Or I guess maybe I'm wasting yours."

"Oh?"

Carolyn looked at the glass between her palms. "I got to thinking about it today. What's the point? Why spend money I don't have, why waste the energy? Like you said, Gregg's gone. Whether he did it or not, what they say—it doesn't matter."

"Kind of a sudden change of heart."

Her shoulders went up and down in a neat roll. "They're determined to make Gregg their scapegoat. The police, I mean. Well, let them. Let them say whatever they want about him. What's the difference? They can't prove anything, or at least they haven't so far."

"And what about you?"

"What about me?" She looked up.

"I thought the whole point was to get the cops off your back."

She angled her hands away from her glass, a palms-out gesture of indifference. "They're going to think and do what they want. Maybe they can't *prove* anything, but neither can I." Suddenly her head became very heavy. It sagged on her long, slender neck. "I just have to wait," she said to the glass in her hands, her voice a ragged, thready whisper. "Just . . . wait. Wait, and try to hang on, and hope they get tired and go away . . ."

"That's some wonderful attitude," I said, looking at her hard. "Well, maybe we *can* do something. At least instill a reasonable doubt, as they say."

Her eyes widened and her body straightened expectantly. "What do you mean? You found out something? Already?"

"Yes and no. Nothing conclusive. Nothing you could call evidence. I can't prove Gregg didn't rob those banks. According to the civics books, it ought to be enough that the cops can't prove he *did*, but we both know how that works." I took a slug of beer. "Look, I can't promise anything, but I do have friends in low places. Might prove helpful if I tell them some things I've learned."

She didn't budge. "Like?"

"Like Gregg's drinking buddies, Abel and Patavena. They profess to know nothing about the alleged larcenies. I believe them. But from what you've said and what I've observed, Gregg and they were pretty tight. Somewhere along the line, probably late one night after a few too many, Gregg was bound to have let *something* slip. He didn't. Which suggests there was nothing to slip."

"What if they were lying? What if they were in on it? What if they have the money?"

"They don't." I laughed.

It was contagious: Carolyn smiled in a confused sort of way and half-laughed, "What's so funny?"

"I'm sorry—but, believe me, if you saw them you'd know what a ridiculous thing you just suggested." I wiped a tear from the corner of my eye. "Besides, when I suggested to them that Gregg may have entrusted his loot to someone else, someone the cops wouldn't know about, the boys immediately scampered off to Ralston to see."

"Who? See who?" Her dark eyes were alive, electric.

I ignored her and drank. The beer tasted like water. "The important discovery, the one the cops would credit, is that Gregg was up to his incisors in debt—"

"*We* were." Haughty. "But I'm working and there's a little insurance and I'm making the paym—"

"—to a private party. A loan shark, they'd call him in the crime novels. Gregg died owing the guy twenty thousand dollars. Which he could have paid off easily if he had seventy-eight grand stuffed into the mattress."

Carolyn looked like I had slapped her. Small wonder: In a way, I had. "I can't believe it," she said hollowly.

"The guy Gregg borrowed the lettuce from isn't a leg-breaker. But he wouldn't have let Gregg go on forever without paying up. Sooner or later you'd have started to notice little things missing from around the house. Like furniture. It behooves you to pay off a guy like that, and Gregg undoubtedly would have if he could have. The fact that he didn't might cut some ice with the proper authorities, as they say in the movies. There's a cop or two I know I can convince: They'll help me with the feds if I need it."

Carolyn's face had been replaced by a pale blank mask of mute shock. Her mouth opened, her lips trembled. She chewed at her bottom lip, wet it with her tongue. Then, hoarsely: "Twenty thousand. What did he do with twenty thousand dollars?"

"Well, the loan really was only ten thousand," I explained. "The rest is interest."

"Dear God." She clasped her hands, forefingers extended, and brought them to her lips. "But what—Where did the money go, the ten thousand . . ."

I pushed the beer can away from me. Suddenly I didn't want any more. "Gambling."

Carolyn seemed to stiffen, slightly, almost imperceptibly. Her voice was cold and the words sounded stilted and rehearsed when she said, "Gregg used to gamble. When we were first married. It was an illness, and he got it treated."

"Well, he should've gone in for a booster shot, because it didn't take. You yourself speculated that the fifty he had on him when he died could have been the product of a pool-hall bet."

"That's not the same thing," she said woodenly.

"No? Just like you're not an alcoholic if all you drink is beer? Or you're not a junkie if your drugs are prescription? Come on, Carolyn. It's not the same thing because you don't want it to *be* the same thing."

She said nothing.

"The man he owed the money to, the loan shark, tells me that Gregg would bet on anything. But even with all that practice he never got any good at it."

Carolyn took a long pull from her glass. Then she sat silently and watched the ice melt in the Cool Whip tub.

I said, "I suppose it's like alcoholism, nicotine addiction, all that stuff. You can be clean for years, then along comes enough stress to shove you off the wagon. Gregg probably *had* quit. But when things got tough . . ." I shrugged. "He probably started with nickel-and-dime stuff, pocket money that he could lose without your noticing. Recreational gambling. Only to a compulsive gambler, 'recreational gambling' is like 'social drinking' to an alcoholic: there's no such animal. Then he must have decided he could win big if he bet big. Another bet would get back his losses . . . *another* one to recoup those . . ."

"Please," she said sourly. "I know the story. I lived through it."

"It's a blessing in disguise, if you want to take the Pollyanna position. If Gregg hadn't been a betting man, he wouldn't have owed the shark twenty grand. If he didn't owe the shark twenty grand, there'd be absolutely nothing, instead of just *practically* nothing, pointing to Gregg's innocence." I fanned my palms in a kind of shrug.

Carolyn raked a hand through the hair covering her left

ear, pulling it back, letting it fall, mussed, behind the ear. Time passed, undisturbed by us. Finally she said, "You really think Gregg was innocent?"

"I don't think he knocked over those banks," I said, which didn't exactly address her question. "Innocence" is for theologians and philosophers. "Not guilty" is for cops and lawyers. And private detectives.

"But I can't prove it," I repeated.

"But you think the police will accept your . . . your theory? That Gregg's owing this man so much money—and not paying it—proves he didn't do it?"

I rubbed an eye, watching her through the other one. "Cops are like everybody else; sometimes they surprise you by their reactions. Sometimes they're off the wall, you can't figure where they're coming from. Mostly, though, cops are mainly reasonable people trying to do a mainly unreasonable job. I can probably convince them. In any event, I think it's worth a try."

Carolyn shrugged and spread her hands on the table, palms down. "Nothing ventured . . ."

"Then that's what I'll do, first thing in the A.M. Which is fast approaching." I stood. "I'd better shove off and let you get some sleep."

"Wait," Carolyn said. She paused, and when she spoke her words were slow, deliberate, controlled. "You said something about how Gregg might have given the money—if there had been any money—to someone else. Who?"

I had hoped she'd forgotten.

I sat again and fiddled with the beer can while I tried to phrase my reply. There are some things that are simply impossible to couch in polite, discreet euphemisms, some things that are simply impossible to break gently. Every cop, public or private, knows this. None of them ever gets any good at telling people that their husband or wife or kid is dead. Any cop you ask will concur.

Telling a woman that her dead husband had been cheating

on her up until the end isn't in the same category, but that doesn't mean it came any easier for me.

Carolyn waited.

I made a last-ditch search for the words. They were nowhere to be found. "All right," I said. "That first time you called me, the time you hung up on the answering machine . . . You told me later you had been thinking of asking me to find out if Gregg was seeing another woman."

"Oh, God," Carolyn said. Emotionlessly. All the emotions had been scoured out of her.

"You were right." I said it as gently as possible, which wasn't gently enough. "For the past few months. Gregg's pal Abel let it slip when I was questioning him. Then I sort of sicced him and Patavena on her so I could follow them."

Carolyn absorbed the news for a minute, maybe more. "What's her name?" she finally said.

"I don't think that's important."

"*I* do," Carolyn snapped. "And I'm the one picking up the tab."

"Then keep your goddamn money." My turn to snap. It was late and I was tired, if that's an excuse. "Use it to hire someone who'll do anything for a buck. Me, I won't. I don't think it'll do you any good to know. Her either. Gregg's gone and the affair is over and I'm not talking. Like it or lump it." Who says I don't have a way with words?

Carolyn glared at me through narrowed eyes, her face flushed, her breathing hard. She was trying to come up with some good ammunition and wasn't having any luck.

Then she was saved by the bell. The doorbell.

Carolyn looked at me, looked at the clock on the stove. "It's a little late for company . . ." she said crossly.

She left the room. I stayed put, trying out sentences in my head. It was hard work, so I got up and went to the sink, took a glass from the shelf above it, and filled it with water from the tap.

At which point I heard Carolyn say, very loudly, "Why can't you people just leave me alone!"

The kitchen had two doors. The door in the south wall led to the dining room; the door in the east wall led past the stairs and into the entryway at the front of the house. I pushed through the second door—it was on a double hinge, like the door Rob and Laura always had so much fun with on *The Dick Van Dyke Show*—and into the entryway.

Standing in the doorway, speaking to Carolyn in low tones, was Bill Jurgenson, junior G-man; his sidekick, Robinson; and three others I didn't recognize. Jurgenson was holding a trifolded paper. I didn't have to read it to know it was a search warrant. Carolyn avoided the paper as if she thought it might be infested.

Jurgenson spotted me and did a neat little double take. I said, "You guys work long hours."

"I was about to say the same about you. Or—" He cocked his head to his left, toward Carolyn.

"Business," I said. I looked at Carolyn. "What's the problem?"

She was agitated. The irritation she'd felt toward me a few minutes ago had now exploded into full-blown, venom-dripping anger. Her eyes were wide, her nostrils flared. Her lips were pulled back away from her teeth and her breath *shoosh*ed between them in quick little gulps. The way she glared at Jurgenson, he might have been something that just climbed up from hell. "He wants to search my house again. He's already done it once, why does he have to bother me again?" She turned her face to me. "Don't let him."

Jurgenson looked at me impassively. To his credit, he didn't fuss or holler or wave his warrant around.

I said, "I don't think there's much that can be done about it, Carolyn." To Jurgenson: "Can't this wait until morning?"

He pursed his lips and gave me a long look. "I'd rather

not." He half-turned and faced Carolyn. "This won't take long, Mrs. Longo."

Carolyn glowered at him, saying nothing. After a few seconds Jurgenson turned to Robinson. The white man nodded almost imperceptibly, and the black man and the others moved to prowl the premises.

"Ironically, I was just telling Carolyn why I thought I could convince you guys to lay off her."

Jurgenson's eyebrows went up. "I'd be interested in hearing that."

"I've come across one or two things that don't prove anything per se, but tend to indicate Gregg Longo must have been innocent."

"I'm still interested." The eyebrows stayed put.

"The most significant of them is Irish Tim."

"Callinan? What's he got to do with this?"

I told him how Gregg Longo was into Callinan for twenty grand.

Jurgenson whistled. "That's a lot of bottle caps. But I don't get your point. A guy owes a lot of money to a legbreaker, seems to me that just makes him a candidate for doing something stupid."

"Stupid would be *not* paying Irish twenty Gs when you have fifty-eight more just like them collecting dust. Longo owed, he did not pay, therefore he did not have the dough, therefore he did not rob the banks. Q.E.D., as they say in the movies."

"Very imaginative." He grinned.

I shrugged. "Talk to Callinan."

Jurgenson's grin widened. "Right. I'm sure he'd be very forthcoming with information."

"Seems to me it'd be more productive than this." I gestured to indicate the house, which Jurgenson's team had begun searching quietly, efficiently. "A little late for fishing, William."

"Some bite at night," Jurgenson murmured. "But this

isn't a fishing trip. When I told you the investigation had been back-burnered, I told you the truth. Things have changed since then."

"Things. What sort of things?"

Carolyn said, "I don't want him here. I don't want these men in this house."

"Carolyn . . ."

"What are you *doing*?" She ran to the black man, Robinson, who had rolled back several feet of rug in the living room and now was tapping at the floorboards with a small rubber mallet. "*Stop that!*" Her voice was harsh and shrill.

Robinson looked at Jurgenson. It seemed like a good idea, so I did too.

Jurgenson moved behind Carolyn and gripped her upper arms in what was meant as a consoling gesture. She pulled away angrily. Jurgenson took a deep breath. "We have to do this, Mrs. Longo," he said to her back. "I'm sorry. We'll be as quick as possible. *And* as careful."

Without a word she stormed out of the room—through the dining room and into the kitchen.

"Damn it, what's going on, Jurgenson? I thought you said you'd take it easy on her."

He slid his glasses back onto his forehead and rubbed his eyes. They were red and watery with fatigue. "Believe it or not, Nebraska, I *am* going easy on her. Have you ever seen a full-scale search? Men all over the place like flies on garbage. This isn't a search. This is nothing. This is— what?—research. Reconnaisance. Inspection . . ."

"Maybe Santa will bring you a nice thesaurus for Christmas," I said irritably. "Meanwhile, what the hell are you *doing* here?"

He repositioned his eyeglasses. "The local banks have been running spot checks for us, comparing serial numbers of the bills they take in against the ones on the bills that were stolen. The ones that we know, at any rate . . ."

"You told me that this afternoon."

"Yeah. What I didn't tell you, I lied when I said none of the money had turned up. We had one the other day. A fifty. We've been working on its trail, tracing it back."

I knew what he was going to say before he said it.

"We traced the note back to a guy named Lou Boyer. He tells us he got the fifty from Gregg Longo."

CHAPTER
ELEVEN

"Tell the truth, now," I said. "Isn't this kind of a big waste of everybody's time?"

We were in the basement, Jurgenson and I, watching one of his minions work. Ordinarily I can stand around all day watching other people work, but tonight I was in no mood for it, giving scant attention to the big-nosed, balding fellow who went quietly about his business.

The basements of old houses are unbeautiful sights. They weren't designed to be potential living space, to someday be turned into rec rooms, bedrooms, or dens, to have saunas or whirlpool baths or pool tables installed at a later date. They were designed to be big holes that you stuck big furnaces in, furnaces that probably burned big quantities of coal that also were stored in, you guessed it, the basement. In that regard, the Longo basement was perfect, a huge, cold hole with uneven concrete floor and rough-hewn cement-block walls. The room was dominated by a colossal thirty-year-old furnace—gas—whose enormous metal tentacles, some round, some square, branched in every direction up toward the house. Other basementy artifacts completed the picture: washer and dryer; water heater; dust-coated cardboard boxes, trunks, and suitcases; a rough-hewn, paint-splattered workbench covered with cans of paint and lacquer and thinner and a thousand other handyman supplies in no discernible order or pattern.

"If it was, I wouldn't be doing it," Jurgenson said evenly. "You think this is my idea of a good time? I have a family, you know, a wife and three kids. At least, I *think* it's three. It's been a long time since I saw them."

It was cold in the basement, and clammy. The temperature had felt refreshing when we first came down, but now the hair on my arms was beginning to rise. "You searched this place before. If the money was here, wouldn't you have found it?"

"I would like to think so. It pays to be sure."

The guy with the nose plucked away the vinyl tape that held an insulating blanket around the water-heater tank, exposing a six-inch strip from top to bottom. He tapped along this strip with the end of his high-intensity flashlight.

"The link to Longo is pretty tenuous. The link to this house, to Carolyn, even more so."

We were standing by the stairs, rough wooden steps in an open staircase, painted industrial gray. Now Jurgenson pushed off and went to breathe down his man's neck. "The trail to Longo is solid," he said. "The fifty-dollar bill was one of three fifties that were part of a regular daily deposit made by one of the Westroads merchants. We talked to the clerks on duty that day; one of them remembered being given a fifty by a man she knew, a man who also worked at the mall. Lou Boyer. We talked to Boyer, who remembered having been given a fifty by Longo just before he died."

"Which is exactly what I would say if the feds were leaning on *me*. I'd tell you guys exactly what I know you want to hear. Especially if I had . . . *neglected* to mention the first time that Longo had paid me a fifty days before he died."

Jurgenson looked back at me, the glimmer of a knowing smile in the red-rimmed eyes behind their lenses. "So he told you about that, huh? Funny, I didn't *quite* believe him when he told me he'd forgotten about the fifty when we interviewed him three weeks ago. A guy might almost think that Longo's buddy was trying to shield him."

"Himself, more than likely." I moved across the concrete floor. "Look, we both know how cash gets around. Just because a store deposits a particular note on a particular day doesn't mean it took in the note on the same day. Maybe it did, maybe the note sat in the store's cash reserve for days or weeks. Boyer's fifty could have been one of the other two in that day's deposit. Or it could be sitting in the store's strongbox right this minute. What I'm getting at is *anyone* could have passed that fifty anytime since it was stolen. Boyer's involvement, such as it is, may be coincidental."

"And maybe not. We have to check it out." Evidently convinced that the tank contained nothing but water, Big Nose drew the ends of the wrap together. Jurgenson held them overlapped while Big Nose pulled the old tape tight across the seam. There was just enough sticky left to hold it together, at least temporarily.

"There's more to it than that, though," I said.

Jurgenson looked at me, wiping his palms together.

"Isn't there?" I pressed. "Your being here, I mean—even if the fifty came from Longo. You think that Carolyn knows something."

He made a dismissive gesture and turned away.

I took his elbow, gave a second's consideration to the look he shot me, and let go. "Sorry," I mumbled. "But I'm right, aren't I? Why else search the place? Again. You think she found the money. Maybe you think she knew where it was hidden all along and's just retrieved it. By having a nice easy look-see here, you're hoping you might notice something out of place, something that's been disturbed since the last time you looked." I pulled my hand across the topmost carton in a nearby stack of boxes and showed my grimy palm. "Like dust. Cobwebs. What do you think? Carolyn knew all along that Gregg was the robber? Hey, maybe she drove the getaway car! Or did she just come across the stash the other day?"

Big Nose threw his light on the cement floor, spidered with cracks that had been amateurishly patched over the decades. The beam drew Jurgenson's and my attention. A large roundish patch, lighter in color than the surrounding floor, caught Big Nose's eye. He crouched and hammered it lightly with the flashlight, across and back in an X pattern. It was solid.

"I don't know," Jurgenson said as if explaining it to a four-year-old. "I don't know if Longo was guilty, but this is the *second* bill from one of the robberies to be linked to him. We have to check. It's the job. You know that."

I rubbed my left eye with the ball of my hand. "Yeah. I know that. It doesn't mean I have to like it."

"Me neither."

"What about Longo owing Callinan twenty grand? What do you think of that?"

Jurgenson reached up overhead and dragged his hand along the top of a cold-air duct. He found dust. "I read this article once about Franklin Roosevelt. Guy who worked for him said that if FDR told you to do something once, you could forget about it. If he mentioned it again, you'd had better give it consideration. If he told you a *third* time, you had better do it." Big Nose had worked his way over to the furnace and was unfastening a front panel. "Irish Tim's the same way. He'll give you about three last chances; it's safe to ignore the first two. Everyone knows it. So if I were Longo, I'd'a waited until my *third* last chance before I paid up. Why give away the money before I absolutely gotta?"

Jurgenson ambled over to the furnace to help his man with the panel, an eight-by-eight square under a chrome legend proclaiming Homart Automatic Heating. I followed. Big Nose worked on four corroded screws with a pocketknife screwdriver while Jurgenson held the panel in place.

"Longo was a small-timer," I said. "Do you really think

he could come into a wad of cash and not throw it around? None of his pals—Abel, Patavena, the Slater woman—none of them gives any indication that Longo was flush when he died."

The last screw defeated, Jurgenson lifted out the steel plate and Big Nose trained his flashlight beam on the interior of the furnace.

"Hell," I said, "Eloise Slater says she loaned him a hundred bucks that he never paid back."

"Things are tough all over." The furnace had been shut down for the summer. It emitted the dusty, disused odor of such things. Jurgenson and friend satisfied themselves that it did not contain seventy-eight thousand dollars, and Jurgenson steadied the metal plate while Big Nose worked the screws back into position. "Look," he said, "why're you telling me all this? What'y'a want from me?"

"Slack. You've got some very tenuous evidence against Longo. I've got some equally tenuous evidence for him. I want you to admit that it's just as likely that Longo *wasn't* dirty—"

"I admit it."

"—to see that even if he *was*, Carolyn Longo didn't and doesn't necessarily have anything to do with it—"

"I see that."

"—and to promise that you'll at least continue to keep an open mind—for Carolyn's sake, not Longo's."

"I promise," Jurgenson said, straightening from his task and stretching his lower-back muscles. "Can I go home now?"

Actually, it was closer to an hour later, give or take, before we closed the front door behind them. Jurgenson apologized to Carolyn again, thanked her for her cooperation, and said he hoped they wouldn't have to bother her further. Carolyn said nothing. Jurgenson shot me a quick look, shrugged with his eyes as much as his shoulders, and tramped onto the porch and out the door. The others followed dutifully, like the Seven Dwarfs.

Carolyn watched until their dark Dodge sedan pulled away from the curb. Then she slammed the front door, double locked it with a vengeance and a skeleton key, and headed purposefully into the kitchen. She fixed a stiff drink, made half of it vanish, and replaced it.

"You would *think* these people would have better things to do than to harass me!"

"Harassment wasn't the point. I won't say there wasn't a little bit of that in there, but it wasn't the point. They could never have gotten a warrant if it had been."

"Bullshit! They ripped this place apart three weeks ago. My husband wasn't even cold yet and they were tearing my *house* apart! They didn't find any money then. What makes them think they'd find it tonight?"

I looked long at her. "They had to check it out. Just to cover the bases."

Carolyn turned on me; her face wore a patina of rage. "Whose goddamn side are you *on*, anyway?" She stormed out of the kitchen via the dining room.

I started to follow her. Hesitated. Took my glass out of the sink, filled it with water, and added a few slivers of ice from the supply floating in the Cool Whip tub. I drank the water and put the glass back in the sink. *Then* I went through the dining room and into the living room, where Carolyn sat uneasily in an easy chair, boring holes through the wallpaper with her dark eyes.

"You think I have the money too," she said hotly.

"Do I?"

"Don't you? Admit it. I don't care. You think what they think, what everybody thinks—that I knew where Gregg hid the money, I've had it all along, I've just been playing it cool."

I flopped on the sofa. "It could be that way," I said. "Is it?"

She turned her eyes away from the wall and searched my face. "No."

"All right."

Her smile was grim. " 'All right'? My say-so's good enough?"

"For me. Why shouldn't it be? Look, Carolyn, I read an awful lot of detective novels, and they're the only place where guilty people hire private investigators because they think it'll make them appear innocent. Real live people don't think that way. They don't bother. Besides, I'd like to think I know you better than that."

She raised her glass two-handed and paused with the rim against her chin. Her eyes looked at something far away. "I'd like to think so too. But I can't say that I haven't thought about all that money, about having it all. With all the bills and everything . . . I don't know. If I went out into the backyard and found a spot where Gregg had buried all that money . . ." Her eyes refocused, sought out mine, found them. "I don't know if I would turn it in or not."

"There's nothing wrong with temptation," I said. "The trouble starts when you give in to it."

"God, though, just to think about it. Ivan, have you ever daydreamed about having stacks and stacks of money?"

"Only constantly. In my dreams, Ed McMahon shows up on the doorstep with a briefcase containing ten million bucks. Actually, you know, Ed doesn't really give you ten million. I think he only gives you something like five-hundred thousand a year for twenty years."

"Gee, what a rip; I'm glad you told me before I wasted twenty-two cents entering. . . . Ivan, if Gregg *did* have all that money, and he hid it away somewhere, and you found it . . . What would you do?"

"This is the second time tonight I've had to think about it," I said. "A smart guy would keep it, go on living in his little apartment and driving his old car, maintain a low profile, improve his standard of living little by little, subtle-like. A smarter guy would skim off twenty or twenty-five thousand and turn the rest over to the cops, letting them think that's all that was left and putting himself well into the clear. Me, being basically chicken and none too smart, I'd probably turn the whole stash over to the badges and politely ask for a receipt."

Carolyn smiled dreamily. "Seventy-eight thousand isn't exactly a fortune," she said, "but it's about four years' pay for me. With seventy-eight thousand dollars we could disappear for a while, at least, Ivan, you and me. Go to Hawaii or Bermuda or someplace." She looked at me. "Pick up where we left off twenty years ago." Her voice matched her smile. "Make up for lost time." She closed her eyes and rested her head against the back of the chair. "Ah, well . . . it's a nice dream." She opened one eye. "And like you said, there's nothing wrong with temptation."

My eyes had been closed; now I opened one and looked at her. "I suspect the odds of your having to wrestle with that particular temptation are slim. Because, as I was saying when we were so rudely interrupted, I do not believe that Gregg ever had that money."

"But— Those men, just now . . ."

"Wishful thinking on their part. They thought it would be nice to waltz in and find where you'd torn up the garage floor, revealing Gregg's stash, which you'd had to tap to pay the paperboy. And it would have been. Nice, I mean. For them. But the problem with cash, and the beauty of it, is that it's largely untraceable." I recapped the conversation I'd had with Jurgenson in the basement, about how the fifty-dollar note attributed to Boyer may easily *not* have been Boyer's at all. "The thing could have been circulating for weeks, months already, before anyone happened to compare serial numbers. The robber buys groceries with it, the grocer gives it in change to a lady who uses it to buy a tank of gas, the service station deposits it in their bank, which doesn't happen to check the number and gives it to a guy cashing his paycheck on his way to the local watering hole. . . . Meanwhile, the crook has been working on his tan in Saint Thomas. The link to you, to Gregg, is about as solid as a cobweb. I wouldn't lose any sleep over it."

"Lou *said* he got it from Gregg."

"Do you suppose Boyer checked the serial number? Do you suppose he put his initials on the bill that Gregg gave him? Boyer has no idea whether the note in question is the one from Gregg. Neither does Jurgenson. Jurgenson's reaching. He reached right out and grabbed Boyer and squeezed hard. Boyer told Jurgenson what he knew he wanted to hear."

Carolyn rested her glass on her right knee, rested her head against the back of her chair, and closed her eyes. She looked exhausted, drained. I shouldn't wonder. Yet there was something enormously attractive about her even so. An appealing vulnerability. She wore a blue denim skirt and a vibrant green shirt with epaulets. Her legs and feet were bare, her sandals carelessly kicked into a corner near the chair.

She opened her eyes and looked at me looking at her.

"You don't do that, Ivan, do you? Tell people what they want to hear?"

"What do you mean?"

She sighed, and closed her eyes again. "You won't tell me her name," she said. "Gregg's . . . girlfriend. Will you tell me what she's like? Do I have a right to know that much at least?"

"What's she like. . . . Twenty-eight, maybe thirty, or thereabout. She's a cocktail waitress. Gregg picked her up, or vice versa, in the bar where she works. They saw each other during the day, when you were at work. Her place. She doesn't think Gregg was guilty, but she doesn't know. She never saw Gregg flash any cash or give any indication that he was in the chips."

Carolyn took a drink, her eyes still closed, her head still

back. "I think I'm supposed to ask what she's got that I
haven't. She's young. Younger than me, anyhow. Is she
pretty?"

"Yes. In some ways she looks like you."

"Maybe I should take that as a compliment." Carolyn
opened her eyes. "Why? I mean, I don't understand. Why,
Ivan?"

"You'd have to ask Gregg." I tried to make it light, gentle,
easy.

"That's not good enough. I don't . . . I need to know,
Ivan. I can't ask Gregg." She looked at me and her eyes
were moist and shining. "I'm asking you."

I ran a hand across the stubble on my chin. "Hell. Even
if you could ask Gregg, I'm not sure he could tell you. I
sure can't. I guess . . . well, evidently she catered to some
of Gregg's, uh, less conventional tastes; maybe that was
it."

She laughed, an unfunny, rather unpleasant laugh. "And
what does *that* mean? Gregg was some sort of pervert?"

"A pervert is just someone who likes to do something
that you don't. Gregg and his friend played little games,
as she put it."

"You dance divinely," Carolyn said sourly. "But what's
your point? Did he like to dress up in women's clothes?
Did he like to screw schoolgirls? Animals? No, he couldn't
stand animals. Can't've been a fag if he was seeing another
woman. What's that leave—whips and chains?"

I looked at her. "Bingo," I said quietly.

The effect, for her, was like running headlong into a brick
wall. "Jesus." It was a bare, hoarse whisper. "Jesus." She
drained her glass. "He never said anything to me. He never
did anything that would make me think . . ."

"I know," I said. "I know." The pointless things you
say to someone who's hurting.

"Jesus." She looked at her empty glass, as if wondering
how it got to be that way. "I need another one. You?" I

shook my head. Carolyn stood, unsteadily, and took two steps toward the dining room. Then she stopped and turned and, without meeting my eyes, softly said, "He could have asked, Ivan. He could have said something. I would have . . . I don't know, he just could have *said* something."

So could I, but at the moment I hadn't the slightest idea what.

Carolyn left the room, left me with my thoughts, left me with my anger at myself for having neither the words to break the news gently nor the finesse to comfort her after breaking it clumsily. Self-anger is difficult to sustain; inevitably, invariably, it turns toward someone else. In this case, Gregg Longo. After all, if he had been faithful to Carolyn—"faithful," that old-fashioned word again—then I would not have been put in the position of having to tell her about her husband's infidelity.

People. Who needs 'em? If there's such a thing as sin, it must be hurting people, nothing more or less complicated than that. What else is there? God? How do you sin against God? You can't hurt him. You can't kill him, you can't swindle him, you can't steal his money, you can't get him hooked on drugs and then turn and put him on the street to pay for his habit. Religious people say you hurt God when you turn away from his word. Which is what? Love thy neighbor.

Self-righteous? All right; what do you expect? Morality is at the center of the job. Any cop, whether he's a private cop or on the public payroll, is a moral policeman. He's fighting the battle of right against wrong, good against evil, order against chaos—all that unhip, uncool, old-fashioned jazz. The beat cop's job is to keep order. The detective's job is to restore order. The private detective's job is to separate order from disorder, to sift through everything and, ideally, find truth. Not justice, necessarily: truth.

And the truth is, sometimes the truth is better left unfound.

I heard water running in the pipes overhead. Carolyn must have slipped through the kitchen and gone upstairs to the bathroom. I listened and soon heard her feet on the stairs.

Carolyn entered the room through the doorway leading to the entry hall. She had washed her face and brushed her dark hair and changed clothes. Now she wore a knee-length white terry robe with blue piping. She did not carry a drink. She carried a long slender piece of gray velvety material that might have been a bathrobe sash.

She crossed the floor and stood with her shins barely touching the footstool in front of me. Her eyes were downcast. Her voice, when she spoke, was ragged. "Tic me," she said softly.

I said nothing. It's what I do when I'm speechless.

Her words came haltingly, as if she had to invent each one before she spoke it.

"I need . . . to feel that someone wants me, really wants me, won't leave me . . ."

I stood and came around the table. I put a hand under her chin and raised her head, but she wouldn't meet my eyes. I kissed her forehead, then her mouth, lightly at first, then more firmly. Her body was warm against mine. She trembled.

She pressed the sash into my left hand. "Tie me," she mumbled. Her breath was hot.

I pushed the robe away from her shoulders. It fell to the floor and she was naked. I kissed her mouth again, and held her as tightly as she held me. Then she pushed away, gently but definitely. She moved away a step and, eyes still downcast, turned and crossed her wrists at the small of her back.

Hesitantly, I looped the sash around her wrists and knotted it loosely.

"Tighter," she whispered.

I reached around her and pulled her to me. Her body

now was very warm—hot—and smooth. My face was in her hair. I breathed the faint scent of her perfume.

"Tighter," she whispered again, insistently.

I reached down to the sash, felt the smooth but nubby texture of it between my fingers. Then I loosened it and let it fall to the floor.

CHAPTER
TWELVE

Mornings after are a bitch, so I did the manly thing and slipped out like a thief in the night while Carolyn was asleep. The world was dark and quiet, the night—morning, rather— was reasonably cool, damp. My car was coated with a layer of fat moisture beads, and a kind of haze formed a corona around the streetlights. It felt like you could grab a handful of air and wring water out of it.

I was in no hurry. I threaded back to my end of town via Sixteenth Street, through downtown, not caring that red lights stopped me at every corner and made me wait for virtually nonexistent traffic to cross. Drunks and hookers and other miscellaneous street denizens competed for side-walk space. Cops cruised the streets, windows down, meaty left arms dangling into space, obscuring the decal on the door. Gaudy pastel neon blinked and buzzed in front of otherwise dark and empty buildings.

I went up Dodge Street, past the old high school where Carolyn and I had first met, all those years ago. Central High is a great, pale, federal-looking building propped atop a rise overlooking the city. At least, overlooking the city as the city must have been when the building went up. It's not the school's fault that most of the city now sprawls out more or less behind and to the west of it.

Past the high school, the Joslyn Museum's banners bally-hooed its Nam June Paik exhibition or display or whatever it was. I had seen it: a wall full of Sony Trinitron television monitors endlessly barraging the viewer with an ever-changing stream of vaguely psychedelic images. When you stepped back from the wall, you saw that the monitors and the images displayed on them conspired to form a collage resembling the American flag, in design if not necessarily colors. I hadn't made up my mind about the exhibition. I know all about art but I don't know what I like.

Past the museum, Vickers bragged about seventy-four-cent gasoline, as if it was something to brag about.

Past the gas station, I got the feeling I was being followed.

I had had the same feeling on the way to Carolyn's house from Irish Tim's little Xanadu. A sexy Ford Taurus had drifted along with me as I headed into the city, sometimes in my rearview mirror, sometimes in my blind spot, for a distance of some miles. Even after I had changed my route and my direction a couple of times. I lost him—or he me—in the tangle of narrow residential streets around the old St. Joe's Hospital, now the Saint Joseph Center for Mental Health, on Dorcas Street. But the jumpy, jittery, prickly feeling of paranoia stayed with me, and I had taken an amazingly circuitous and gasoline-wasting route to Carolyn's place.

I had convinced myself that the only thing following me was coincidence—after all, we wouldn't need so many streets in the burg if a lot of people didn't drive on them a lot, sometimes several people at the same time, on the same street, going the same direction. But now the edgy feeling was coming back, strongly.

Let's put things in perspective, I told myself. Outside of the imaginations of television producers and crime novelists, people rarely get followed. Excuse me: "tailed" is the preferred jargon. It happens, of course—it's happened to me, and I've caused it to happen to a dozen or more people over the years—but it doesn't happen so frequently that it gets monotonous. Which is lucky, since it's very difficult to determine with certainty whether you are in fact being followed. Tailed.

And it pays to be sure. Several years ago I lured a "shadow" onto a narrow side street, jammed my car edgewise across the road, grabbed my revolver from the glove compartment, leaped out like Captain America . . . and nearly gave heart attacks to an elderly couple who only wanted to let me know I'd lost a hubcap to a pothole several blocks back.

At night, the problem of certainty is greater. You've seen one set of headlights, you've pretty well seen 'em all.

Past Twenty-fifth Street, the traffic on Dodge grew slightly heavier, which would only make life easier for someone tailing me. Heavy traffic and no traffic make for hard shadowing. Light-to-medium makes it a snap.

Without signaling, I turned right past the Amoco at the bottom of the hill and gunned the Impala up the freeway ramp. As I turned I hit the tiny lever under the rearview mirror, canting it up from its glare-killing night-driving position, brightening the picture. In the cold, harsh light spilling from the service station I could see that the suspect car was a dark blue or black sedan. I didn't get a make before I hit the ramp.

I'd have another chance, however. The car mimicked my turn.

I ignored the speed limit on the North Freeway, whipped past Creighton University and down the exit ramp to Burt Street. The Chevy's engine wailed in outrage at the unaccustomed abuse. At Burt I signaled for a left turn, the only kind they let you make there, but jumped the red and went straight, up the hill, looping through an apartment-complex parking lot and reemerging on the hill, facing the intersection

I'd just bulled through. I drifted over to the curb and doused
my headlights.

The sedan, a Lincoln, I could now see, sat at the light
on the other side of the intersection, signaling for a left.

The light went green and the Lincoln made the turn. I
let up on the brake pedal, rolled into the intersection, and
turned right to follow it, leaving the headlights black.

Whoever was behind the big car's wheel didn't seem to
be in any hurry—didn't seem to be rushing to try to find
me. Past Thirtieth, Burt merges with Cuming Street, and
the intersection is lighted up like an operating theater. There
was no longer any point in sailing along without lights, so
I pulled the switch on the dashboard and continued to hold
back four or five car lengths.

The sedan turned left onto Fortieth Street. By that point
I was certain that the driver had just happened to follow
the same route as me. Well, okay, ninety percent certain.
I continued west on Cuming, followed the northward curve
onto the Radial, and let the highway take me the eight
blocks home.

I got to Decatur Street shortly before the hour I should
have been getting up. I left off the lights, except for the
fluorescent doughnut over the kitchen sink, which I needed
while I threw together a pot of coffee. I poured a cup and
went out through the sliding doors and onto my so-called
balcony, which is about the size of a piece of notepaper.

A six-foot square of pavement was missing from the darkened street below, exposing the ancient cast-iron gas fittings
that lay six or eight feet beneath street level. The city was
ripping them up all over town, replacing the old works with
spiffy new ones made of plastic or PVC or fiberglass or something equally sexy that probably cost more than the old
material but would only last half as long. Your tax dollar at
work.

An orange-and-white sawhorse barricade guarded the
wound in the pavement. The sawhorse was topped with

two blinking yellow lights. One of the lights was sick and
the other was dying. They blinked out of sequence as I
watched them, mesmerized, for several moments. Then one
of them speeded up or the other slowed down—I don't
know which—and their blinks grew closer together. The
yellow light seemed to jump from the right-hand lamp to
the left-hand lamp. Faster and faster. Then they blinked
in sync awhile. Then the light appeared to leap from left
to right. Then they were hopelessly out of sequence again.

If it's late enough and you're weary enough, phenomena
such as that can take on deep significance.

Uninvited, Jennifer came into my thoughts.

Jennifer. My wife.

When you thought about it—and I didn't very often—
my marriage was a lot like my private-eye career: I still
had the paperwork, and every once in awhile, as circumstance
dictated, I fooled around with it, but when the inky, heavy
night pressed in and I was alone with myself and too tired
to keep up the pretense, the pointlessness of it all settled
on me with all its crushing weight. Jennifer and I were
like the warning lamps—occasionally synchronized but eventually, inevitably, back out of step, out of whack, out of
. . . out of everything.

I slurped too-hot coffee and leaned against the iron railing.
It was cool and damp.

Gregg Longo cheated on Carolyn with Eloise Slater. I
cheated on Jen with Koosje. Jen cheated on me with I'll
never know how many men in how many corners of the
world. I cheated on Koosje with Carolyn.

My self-righteous dissertation on honor and sincerity, fidel-
ity and truth and justice and the American way—it all echoed
hollowly in my brain now, and I felt mildly ill.

I poured the coffee over the rail and listened to the brittle
sound of it splashing onto the pavement a story below.

I had been truthful when I told Koosje that I wanted to
sleep with Carolyn and then get up in the morning and

have it not have been. Have my cake and eat it too, I had said—or, more accurately, eat it and still have it. I wanted the pleasure of sleeping with my old flame without hurting the relationship with my new flame.

Put more succinctly, I was no better, no more righteous, no more faithful than Gregg Longo had been.

In the far distance, to the southwest, lightning fluttered against the sky, like the phosphors you see when you squeeze your eyes shut tight. There was no thunder. Too far away. When we were kids we had some kind of formula for telling how far away lightning was. We counted the seconds between the time we saw the flash of the lightning and the time we heard the sound of the thunder. I couldn't remember the formula anymore. I never knew if it was valid or not.

I like a good electrical storm. Something about the display, the demonstration of raw, naked elemental force, the sheer wildness of it appeals to me. Out here, we get electrical storms like none I've ever seen anyplace else, not even elsewhere in the Midwest. Great crackling bolts, not mere flashes of light but jagged blue *bolts* ripping across the sky, accompanied by sharp, terrible claps of thunder that sound like cannon fire in your ears and thump way down in your chest and make you jump. The very atmosphere is super-charged with excitement—literally, electricity—and for one sizzling instant you know how Clark Kent must feel when he steps out of that phone booth.

Tonight the lightning was far away. We'd see none of it, beyond this weak lightening of the distant horizon.

Tired but not sleepy, I locked up, killed the kitchen light, and toddled down the hall to my bedroom. I sat at my desk, put on the lamp, and looked at my typewriter, a pale blue Smith Corona Coronet, the kind with the pop-out ribbon cartridge. At the rate I was going, one cartridge would last . . . oh, years and years. I stared at the yellow paper wrapped around the roller, read and reread the half-dozen lines typed there.

Then I yanked the paper out of the machine, balled it up and tossed it, and inserted a fresh sheet of white bond.

I began pecking out my report to Carolyn Longo.

That's what you do when a case is over.

CHAPTER
THIRTEEN

The sun came up and made things Thursday. I had fallen into an unrestful sleep on the living-room sofa, fully clothed, and felt the way you're supposed to feel when you fall asleep on the living-room sofa fully clothed. I forced myself into a semi-upright position, mentally assessed the bruises, scrapes, and sore muscles left over from yesterday's two-step with Abel and Patavena, dumped out the night's cold coffee, and went about fixing a replacement batch. I showered, and shaved in the shower, and brushed my teeth for a long time in the shower. Then I got dressed and drank most of the coffee and ate two old English muffins that were okay once I cut the moldy spots away, and felt better.

Probably as a result of the mold. Penicillin, you know.

When the blood supply to my brain had been restored, I got on with the day.

Loverboy went to work and I went with him.

Then I stashed the car and scouted out Kim Banner. She was sitting behind her desk and an Egg McMuffin. I said, "Why don't you hang out at a doughnut shop like every other cop," and she made a face at me.

I sat and sipped gingerly at the Styrofoam cup I had filled

from the coffeepot in the bull pen. "Got something for you,"
I said.

"Please," Banner said. "Can't you see I'm eating?"

"About Gregg Longo."

Banner leaned back in her creaky chair and lifted her
own coffee cup, a space-capsule-shaped "tipless" mug that
had Holiday Inn and a toll-free reservations number on the
side. "Why me? This isn't my case. My squad has nothing
to do with it. The *division* hardly has anything to do with
it. I'm not interested. I don't care. Yet somehow you and
the feds both think I should be in on the deal."

"We know how hurt you'd be if we left you out."

"I wouldn't. Honest."

"Aw, you don't have to put on the brave front with me.
Listen, all I want you to do is plant a bug in the right
ears."

"Which ears? I'll point 'em out to you and you can do
your own planting."

"I don't know which ears. That's why I need you." The
coffee had the burned taste that is almost inevitable with
thirty-six-cup urns. Percolation is no way to make coffee.
"Here's the lowdown," I said, and told Banner all about
Gregg Longo and Irish Tim Callinan and why I felt strongly
that the former owing the latter twenty Gs meant the latter
didn't have in his possession seventy-eight Gs. You've heard
the whole business a couple of times now already; there's
no point going over it again.

Twenty minutes later Banner, who had been staring in-
tently at a Ticonderoga pencil lodged point first in a ceiling
tile overhead, said, "If Longo didn't bust the banks, who
did?"

"Could be anybody," I said.

"Longo's car was placed at the scene of at least one
holdup," Banner said.

"A car *like* his, *maybe*, was *possibly* seen. The I.D. isn't
what you'd call rock solid."

"His whereabouts at the times of the robberies are unaccounted for. You said even his girlfriend can't vouch for him."

"*My* whereabouts are unaccounted for, too. People who don't need alibis don't go out of their way to line them up. I'd be more suspicious of Longo if his little playmate could produce a calendar showing that he was with her on every date and at every time in question. Wouldn't you?"

She ignored it. "What about that fifty-dollar note?"

"What about it? It could have been circulating for weeks before it hit a bank—it could have gone through several banks before it hit one that happened to be spot-checking serial numbers. Hell, the robber could've tipped an airport skycap with it on his way *out* of town following his last holdup."

"Sure, Sherlock. Just like it *could* be that Longo paid his buddy with money from the robbery."

"That would be brilliant. And then why didn't Longo pay Boyer all of the money he owed? Why didn't he pay Eloise Slater? Why didn't he pay Callinan?"

"You're right—it would be a stupid thing to do, but people do stupid things all the time. Borrowing money from loan sharks is stupid. Robbing banks is stupid. Maybe Longo *was* stupid. Maybe he was careless. And maybe he was a crook, which is why he didn't keep current with his debts."

"Do you buy that?"

Banner sighed elaborately and ran a hand through her short, dirty-blond hair. "No. Stupid is one thing, suicidal is something else. . . . All right, Nebraska. I don't know if it'll do any good, but I'll spread the word. What about the feds, though, are you straight with them?"

I shrugged. "Jurgenson's about like you. Skeptical, but reasonable."

"That's about the nicest thing anyone's said to me all day."

I stood. "Gorilla dust," I said.

"I beg your pardon?"

"Gorilla dust. When gorillas fight, they grab handfuls of dust from the ground and throw them up into the air to blind and confuse each other. That's all this is—gorilla dust. Nobody knows anything. Nobody can prove anything. All we're doing, all of us, is throwing dust into the air, confounding and distracting each other, hoping the other gorilla will get tired first and give it up. It's a completely unsatisfactory way to resolve things. Us P.I. types like to wrap these things up in a hail of bullets that, remarkably, miss us but take out the evildoers."

"Welcome to reality," Banner said. "You gotta find the evildoers before you can take 'em out."

Koosje's office is over a French bakery in the Old Market. The Old Market is what the name indicates: an old market, the old city market, to be precise, where grocers and restaurateurs and food suppliers once argued and haggled and swore at one another in the predawn on a daily basis. Now it's a tourist trap, albeit a charming one, with its red-brick buildings and its cobblestone streets, its sometimes painfully trendy shops and cafés and its seemingly infinite supply of junk masquerading as antiques.

Koosje's operation is through a door coated with ancient royal-blue paint that is badly alligatored. The door leads to a long set of stairs so steep and narrow it might as well be a ladder. At the top is a landing slightly smaller than an LP-record jacket and a door, unpainted. On the door is a wooden plaque with gold lettering: Koosje Van der Beek, Ph.D, and below it, Psychologist. The door opens to a small, high-ceilinged, sparsely decorated reception room, off of which there are two larger rooms where Koosje sees patients, or "clients," as she prefers to call them. The northern room's door was closed; the southern room's door was six or eight inches ajar.

Cinda—not "Cindy"; blame her parents—looked up in mild surprise. I never drop by unannounced.

"She's with someone," Cinda said apologetically.

"Just let her know I'm here, okay?"

The girl picked up the phone and I picked up last month's *Smithsonian*. No old *Reader's Digest*s and *People*s and *Golf*s lying around with stickers on their tattered covers threatening you with unspecified curses if you swiped them, as if you would want to. Koosje's waiting-room literature runs more to *Smithsonian* and *The New Yorker*, *American Heritage* and *Connoisseur*. Several of the Time-Life books about flying graced a small walnut bookcase. People who enjoy flying are relaxed by pictures depicting flight, Koosje says, and people who don't like flying won't look at the books in any case.

"Why don't you go ahead and wait in the other room, if you like," Cinda said, nodding toward the open door. I moved off just as she spoke into the mouthpiece, announcing me.

The wait was short. Through luck rather than good planning, I had happened by at around a quarter before the hour, just five minutes or so before Koosje's sessions usually end. I hadn't even finished "Around the Mall and beyond" when the connecting door slid open and Koosje stepped in. She wore a light gray pin-striped suit and a pink blouse with a tall, narrow collar—the kind Herbert Hoover's always wearing in the old pictures. Of course, Hoover never wore his with an eighteen-inch string of pearls. At least, he never let himself be photographed wearing them.

"This is a surprise," she said. "Or did you tell me you'd be by and I forgot?"

"No," I said, "this is completely impromptu."

"Mm." She sat in one of the two Scandinavian-style chairs near the sofa I was seated on. This was the "informal" room; the other, Koosje's office, was a little more authoritarian. That room looked a lot like a dean's office, this room looked a lot like somebody's living room. Koosje's, come to think of it.

She said, "Is everything all right?"

I said, "Yeah," and filled her in about recent events.

"That sounds good," Koosje said when I had finished. "Why do you look like you just swallowed a lemon?"

"Because I don't like it when things just *hang,* as they are now. Because I like conclusions, resolutions." I looked at her. "Because I slept with Carolyn Longo last night."

Koosje nodded, her eyes on mine. "Why are you telling me?"

"Because you have a right to know. I know there's a school of thought that holds that the errant partner should never ever tell the injured party, but I'm not sure I buy into that."

"Mm. I have counseled married clients to do just that— *not* tell their spouses about an affair. It only hurts the spouse. It doesn't undo the injury." She sighed. "But they usually tell all anyway. They're looking for forgiveness. They want to be told it's all right. Or they want to be told it's *not* all right and get thrown out of the house. Either way, the burden is off of them, off of their consciences." Her eyes wandered the room and returned to my face. "Is that what *you* want, Nebraska? Forgiveness?"

"I don't know. Maybe. As I said, I'm a guy who likes resolutions."

Koosje stood and walked over to the tall windows in the west wall. She looked down at the street below. "We're not married. We've made no promises. I told you before."

"No explicit promises," I said. "But I guess I always felt . . ."

"I did too." She turned. The light was behind her: I could not see her face. "Now what? I told you how I felt and you told me how you felt, and you went and did what you did, which is your right, and now you've come here and you've eased your conscience. You've put the responsibility on me. *I* have to decide what happens next. What am I supposed to do?"

"I don't know."

"I don't either." Her voice was steady and calm. We might as well have been discussing whether to get a toaster fixed or to scrap it and buy a new one. Partly that was Koosje's nature. Partly it was her professional training. And partly it was the surroundings. They were designed and decorated to be calming, soothing, nonthreatening. I hadn't chosen the location with that in mind, but if it helped, so much the better.

"What is there between you and Carolyn?" Koosje asked.

"Twenty-year-old memories. An unfinished love affair."

Koosje let go a puff of air that might have been a short laugh. "Is that it? An unfinished case that you had to wrap up? Just another search for resolution?"

"Could be. Look, I told you before, I'm not entirely in touch with what's going on between me and Carolyn. Maybe nothing. I do know that when I rolled out this morning it was *you* I wanted to see, not her."

"Because your conscience bothered you."

"All right. Would it be better if it hadn't? Would it be better if I didn't care one way or the other? Maybe I'm here right now because, subconsciously, I want you to tell me it's okay I went to bed with another woman last night. Maybe, subconsciously, I want you to break off the relationship. Or maybe I'm here because the whole *point* of a relationship is trying to figure out what makes the other person tick. How can we have a relationship if you don't have—if I don't give you—what you need in order to try to understand me better? And vice versa. That's why Jen and I don't have a relationship. Neither one of us has the slightest idea where the other one is coming from.

"So, yeah, I could have kept mum about sleeping with Carolyn. I would feel guilty, but you get over that, you learn how to handle that. I could have kept you in the dark and we would go on much as before. But there would be a flaw. And the flaw would be that I had not been honest with you. I would have lied to you about *me*, about what I am. Why? So you would keep loving me? What you would be loving, though, would be the lie. You might not know it, but I would. And it would have its effect.''

I stood up and walked across the room, stood next to her and looked down at the street, at the diagonally parked cars, at the tourists, and the locals escorting their out-of-town guests. Koosje's eyes were on me. I could feel them. After a little while I turned and faced them. They were clear and dry and almost dispassionate, almost disinterested.

Almost, but not quite.

"Sooner or later," I said, "it would have its effect. I thought sooner would be better. Bad enough I've hurt you, something I never wanted to do; I won't compound the sin by lying to you.''

I watched the street awhile. Koosje turned toward the window and did likewise.

"What about you and Carolyn?''

"The sixty-four-thousand-dollar question. I don't know. I guess it depends on you. On whether you think we, you and I, have a future. That's not to say I'll turn right around and take up with Carolyn if this is the end for you and me, just that if there is a future for you and me, I want to be in on it.''

Koosje remained mute, watching the street.

"I do know this," I said. "The other night you asked why I would want to risk losing what we have, you and I. I didn't answer. Now I *have* risked it. And having risked it . . . I keep asking myself the same damn question.''

Koosje said nothing. I said nothing.

And we stood there for some time, watching people who didn't know they were being watched, saying nothing.

CHAPTER
FOURTEEN

In case you haven't guessed, I let Loverboy lunch in peace.
I didn't leave Koosje's office until after twelve, just in time
to make her late for her noontime group, and by the time
I got downtown Jonathon Desotel would already have gone
in search of the perfect hamburger with fries. He had never
dined at the Olympic Club during the time I was on his
tail. Whether that was a commentary on the cuisine or merely
indicative of Desotel's need for a midday change of scenery,
I couldn't say.

Oh, sure, I probably could have tracked him down if I'd
really wanted to. I'm a trained detective and everything—
plus Desotel was in the habit of hitting the same downtown
bars and beaneries with numbing regularity. Or I could have
camped in front of the club and awaited his return, just to
reassure myself that he was sticking to the routine. But
the sad truth is, I didn't feel like it. I had practiced being
his shadow for more than a week; I had gotten quite good
at it; and I was bored with it. The nonresolution of the
Longo business aggravated me, bothered me, like an itch
you can't reach. I couldn't let it go. I couldn't concentrate
on anything else. And I couldn't shake the feeling that it

was more than a little strange that the Longo affair and the Desotel affair overlapped, the point of overlap being Eloise Slater and Jonathon Desotel's mutual acquaintance.

I swung by the Central Library, found a meter with forty minutes left on it, and went up.

After I don't know how many years, I still wasn't used to the "new" library. Libraries are supposed to be *old* buildings, cramped, hushed, poorly lighted, musty, smelling of book dust and wood floors and the flowery, old-fashioned perfume of the wizened crones behind the circulation desk. They are *not* supposed to be open, airy, well-lighted spaces filled with glass and gray steel, resonating with activity, loaded with electronic gimcrackery. For cryin' out loud, they don't even stamp book cards anymore. They take a *picture* of it lying next to your library card.

It ain't natural.

I dug up some local directories, city as well as telephone, and looked up Jonathon Desotel's—and Eloise Slater's— backward-named friend. The name had been sort of rattling around in the old brainpan ever since the Slater woman first mentioned it. I didn't know why. James didn't look at all familiar to me, and I was certain we had never met. Of course, as I said before, I do get around some and could have come across the name anywhere. Or, hell, maybe I was thinking of the fifth president of these United States.

The city directory gave Monroe James's occupation as "financial consultant," which I already knew and which was about as unhelpful a description as could be imagined. If I advise you not to put fifty cents in a broken vending machine, does that make me your "financial consultant"?

His home address was listed. No office address.

The white pages gave an office number beneath his residential listing but, again, no address.

James carried only a line listing in the Yellow Pages, no display ad. Again, no street address, just James, Monroe, Fin Cnslt and the Omaha number. I tried comparing the prefix and the number against those of the consulting firms listed, in case he worked out of one of them. No match.

Too bad. I would have liked to visit his office. Whether or not the man was in.

The pay phones were downstairs. I invested money in one and dialed James's office. "This is Monroe James. I'm not available right now—"

I slammed down the receiver hook, breaking the connection, and shoved a finger into the coin-return slot. I once read in a Lawrence Block novel that if you hang up on an answering machine fast enough, sometimes you get your money back. It's never worked for me.

They do a pretty fair job of hiding the *World-Herald* index, but with the help of a librarian—young, well dressed, nice looking, and male: not at all as God intended—I found it. And James, Monroe.

There were perhaps a dozen entries, none of them more recent than three years, most of them ganged up over a four- or five-month span, some of them daily in that time.

OMAHA LAWYER FACES CHARGES

NEW QUESTIONS IN REILLY JURY-BRIBE CASE

LOCAL LAWYER QUESTIONED IN JURY-TAMPER CASE

LAWYER CENSURED

LAWYER JAMES DISBARRED

JAMES CHARGES DROPPED

"Lawyer James Disbarred" sounded promising. I got hold of the proper microfilm spool—plastic newspapers: more blasphemy!—and wheeled to the last page of the local-news section, four years back:

LAWYER JAMES DISBARRED

From staff reports

LINCOLN—Omaha lawyer Monroe James yesterday was disbarred by the Nebraska Bar Association. James, who has been accused of jury tampering in the recent trial

of former Omaha Councilman Rob Reilly, had been censured by the association last April.

A reporter's calls to James yesterday were not returned.

Katherine Gallagher of the state bar association said
disbarring would not affect criminal charges pending
against James. . . .

I didn't care what Katherine Gallagher said. I skimmed
to the bottom of the piece:

James, 39, has long been a controversial figure in trial
law. He had been associated with several Omaha law
firms, most recently Miller Moore Gianelli and Feeny.

Miller Moore Gianelli and Feeny—no commas, puh-*leez*—
was one of those brash, aggressive, balls-to-the-walls firms
that have been springing up everywhere in the last ten or
fifteen years. No erudite gentlemen in three-piece pinstripes
and pince-nez, these: Miller Moore, et al., were to their
bar what brawlers are to mine. Combat lawyers. As near as
I could tell, they had never shunned publicity, or notoriety,
before. If they dumped James, and reading between the
lines said they had—well, that was interesting.

As was the fact that Miller Moore Gianelli and Feeny
was the firm that employed Carolyn Longo.

Miller Moore occupied a substantial chunk of a midtown
office center. It was all industrial carpet, fabric-covered walls,
modern art, lots of glass. An almost clinical sterility. The
library was a narrow room, as underfurnished as the reception
area had been, and dominated by a chrome-legged long
table whose ebony surface was polished to a mirror brilliance.
Chrome shelving on two walls supported uncounted tons
of legal volumes. Sunlight slipped in through quarter-inch
gaps in the blinds over two long windows.

Carolyn was late coming back from lunch. The receptionist

was certain she'd be back any minute. I always wonder, when people say things like that, how they know. In any event, I accepted her invitation to wait in the library, declined her offer of coffee. My caffeine-intake rate goes in cycles, and I had been on a definite upturn lately. Time to taper off again. Or risk being drummed out of the Robert Young Fan Club.

I didn't have a report for Carolyn. The one I had started on in the wee hours rested, unfinished, in my typewriter. It seemed like everything I started lately remained unfinished. *Unfinished Business*, I thought. That's what I should title The Next Book. Assuming I ever finish it, of course. But with Carolyn's report, at least, I had a valid reason: Monroe James. Midway into the report, or less, I realized that James's acquaintance—or whatever—with Eloise Slater connected him at least tenuously to the Longo investigation. Until I had followed up on that connection, whatever the follow-up might or might not reveal, a report was premature.

"Unfinished business," I said to the books along the wall.

Carolyn finally showed, flushed and somewhat breathless. Her dark hair was mussed, as if she hadn't taken the time to stop and brush it after coming in from the great outdoors.

"Sorry," she said. "You should have let me know you were coming, I'd've been sure to be here and—"

"It's all right. Spur-of-the-moment kind of thing. If this isn't a good time . . ."

"No, it's fine. I've just been behind schedule all day, is all. I had a hard time getting out of bed this morning." She tried a tentative, almost shy smile. "When you were gone this morning, I didn't . . ." She paused, closed the library door, and leaned against it. "Were you turned off by . . . you know . . ."

Talk like this always makes me uncomfortable, fidgety. No matter what you say, it's the wrong thing. Or the inflection's wrong. Or it's taken wrong. Now you know why I had ducked the morning-after scene that A.M. Only to voluntarily walk into an afternoon-after scene. "Did I act turned off?" When in doubt, answer with a question.

Her smile grew slightly. "Not very." She smoothed her hair self-consciously. "I don't know what happened last night, Ivan, I really don't. I don't know what came over me. When you told me about Gregg and his . . . well, his girlfriend and the things they liked to do, I—I don't know. I can't explain it, I can't explain why I wanted you to . . . tie me up. Or thought I did. I'm not the sort who fantasizes about whips and chains and dungeons—all that *Story of O* stuff."

"There's a considerable difference between a little innocent B and D and having someone's initials branded on your backside," I said.

"How . . . how far do you think Gregg and his friend went?"

"Pretty far, from what I gather. She has all the paraphernalia."

Carolyn shuddered a little. Maybe it was because the air-conditioning was cranked up too high. She started to speak, lost her voice or her momentum. Again she smoothed her hair and the front of her dress in a nervous, self-conscious way. Her eyes were not on me. "Thanks," she finally managed.

"For what?"

Another search for the words.

"For not . . . I was confused last night. Or something. Thanks for not taking advantage of that. Thanks for . . . Well, just thanks."

Carolyn's eyes found mine. There was something in them, something to be read, but it was written in a language I didn't understand. There was a part of me that wanted to spend a lifetime learning that language.

I cleared my throat, mumbled something inane in response to her thanks, cleared my throat again once or twice, and, finally, said, "I need to ask you about someone. He used to work here. Monroe James."

Maybe I was just projecting—you pick up neat jargon like that when you hang around with shrinks—but Carolyn seemed almost as eager as I was to have the subject changed. We were good midwesterners, uncomfortable putting our deepest feelings into words and laying them out for others to see. I guess I should speak only for myself. But Carolyn showed no signs of objecting to a new topic. "Him," she said, rolling her eyes elaborately.

"Then you know him."

"*Knew* him. Sort of. I never worked with him directly, thank God."

"Bad egg?"

"James was a hot dog, a grandstander. Everyone here is, more or less—the firm has that reputation, and the attorneys love it and play it up as much as possible—but James was different. He was lazy. Good, but lazy. He used these shyster tactics to cover up the fact that he was too lazy to do his homework. He cut corners, took risks he didn't have to take. Guys like him spend twice as much energy trying to get out of doing the job right as they'd spend just doing it. You know they kicked him out of here? That's pretty heavy-duty, especially with someone who'd probably have made partner in another year or two."

"He was disbarred, too."

Carolyn nodded. "And escaped prosecution by a hair's breadth, or so the jungle drums said."

"What exactly did he do? Something about jury tampering . . ."

She had been standing. Now she pulled out a chrome-tube chair with pale gray upholstery and sat. I hitched a hip up onto the edge of the conference table. It was like sitting on a block of ice.

"They say he bribed a juror in that Reilly trial a few years ago." She shrugged. "No one was able to prove anything, so the charges were dropped."

"And so was James."

"I don't think there was any question but that he did it. Proving it was something else again. Of course, the irony is Reilly got sent up anyway."

My recollection of that case was dim, very dim. Something about misappropriation of city property and services—he had a municipal road crew resurface his driveway, or something equally weighty. I couldn't remember exactly, still can't, and don't care enough to go back and look it up. Events like that are of their time: much in the news today, the topic of every conversation no matter how casual; tomorrow, faded like cut flowers.

"Have you seen Monroe James since he left the firm?"

Carolyn frowned at me. "That's an odd question."

My turn to frown. "How so?"

"I told you I hardly knew him."

"You know an awful lot about him."

"Office talk—the jungle drums. I barely knew the man."

"But have you seen him lately? Talked to him?"

"Why are you cross-examining me?"

"Come on, Carolyn, you've hung around lawyers enough to know this isn't cross-ex. I'm just asking a question."

"Why? What's Monroe James got to do with anything?"

Good question, I thought.

"Good question," I said. "I'm trying to figure that one out myself. I keep tripping over James, peripherally, sort of."

"What, did he have something to do with Gregg?" Her dark eyes were very wide, inquisitive.

"No, I don't think so. This is another case entirely." Now it was my turn to dodge the question. "But I figured, since James used to work here, maybe you could tell me a thing or two about him. Do you know what he's doing now?"

"Haven't the slightest idea. I could maybe find out . . ."

"That's okay, I'm sure I can, too, if it's important."

"You're sure? Someone here's bound to know . . ."

"No, it's all right." Someone there *was* bound to know,

probably, but I didn't need that someone alerting James to the fact that a private investigator had been in asking about him. It would spoil the surprise. Whatever the surprise was going to be. "Thanks anyhow."

I slid off the end of the table. Carolyn got to her feet. "Will I see you later?"

I looked at the books on the shelves behind her. "I've sort of been seeing someone else, Carolyn."

"Oh. Is it serious?"

"You make it sound like an illness. Yes, it's serious. Serious enough. I don't want to do anything to damage it. I don't want to hurt her. And I think maybe I did both of those things already."

She turned her back to me, as if scanning the same dry, ponderous volumes that my eyes had gone to when I couldn't face her. "Oh," she repeated. "Then last night . . ."

So we were back to that again. "Last night was last night. You said you don't know what happened. Well, neither do I. You needed something and I needed something, and we found it. You needed to feel cherished, possessed, whatever. I needed to conclude something that had begun twenty years ago."

"That *ended* twenty years ago." She turned and faced me and her eyes were red and moist and shiny. "Ended. Last night was the beginning of something *new*."

"Carolyn." I took her by the shoulders. "Carolyn, I'm sorry, I don't think so."

She pushed away. "You were whistling a different tune last night in the sack."

There was no point arguing with her. She had an unfair advantage: the truth. I moved toward the door.

"Wait."

I did, and felt her hand on my shoulder, cool through my thin cotton shirt.

"Ivan, I'm sorry. That was cruel. I . . . well, you're right. I needed something last night, and you provided it. I had hoped maybe you and I would get back on track again. But I think I knew all along we never would. We've been off-track too many years, maybe. I don't know."

I had turned. Now I took her into my arms, smelled the warm, fresh perfume of her hair, felt her generous body against me. "Damn it," I said. "If things had been different . . . twenty years ago . . . today . . ."

Carolyn ended the embrace and stepped back, wiping her eyes with her fingertips. "Things *aren't* different. It's no good wishing they were."

"No. I guess not."

There was what the novelists call an awkward silence. Suddenly we both found the carpet extraordinarily fascinating.

Finally Carolyn spoke, with a self-deprecating half-laugh. "You were my first love, Ivan, did you know that? Oh, it sounds silly now, but back then . . . I used to think of us as Romeo and Juliet, you know, star-crossed lovers. Very tragic, very romantic." She touched my cheek, very delicately. "I guess I still think of us that way." Then she took her hand away and turned, this time toward the shaded windows. "Well, at least we're friends again, right?"

"Right," I said lamely.

"Okay." She snuffled wetly. I may have snuffled a little myself. She turned toward me again. "Um, say, did you happen to talk to the police? About Gregg . . ."

"Oh. Yeah. This morning. I told them all about Gregg and the money he owed, the money he could have paid back if he'd knocked over those banks."

"Uh-huh. And?"

"And now we do what is commonly known as waiting and seeing. The cop I spilled it to promised to pass it along to them what should have it passed along to them. The feds already know: I told Jurgenson all about it last night. Now the various interested parties have to mull it over and decide what is and is not worthwhile. Personally, from what

I've seen, they have so little to tie Gregg into the thing that I think they'll probably be glad of any excuse to drop him entirely."

"God, I hope so." She sniffed again and rubbed her nose. "I need to get on with my life."

"Well," I said after a while, "I think there's a light at the end of the tunnel."

She barked a harsh, humorless laugh. "You know the joke—that light at the end of the tunnel is a train coming at you."

CHAPTER
FIFTEEN

The afternoon, uncomfortably warm, uncomfortably stuffy, stretched out before me. I drove around awhile in a futile effort to cool off and sort things out. I cased Monroe James's neighborhood, trying to figure out what to do about him, how to handle him. It was a nice day for a little breaking and entering, but the environs were a little too busy for my tastes. Too many kids. Kids'll do you in every time. Whenever events call for sneakiness, you can count on attracting a kid like a picnic attracting ants.

I decided to see what my subconscious could do with the problem, and put a few more miles on the odometer.

Eventually my not-so-happy wandering brought me near the old Decatur Street homestead, and my potbelly reminded me that it hadn't been stoked lately.

The mail wasn't anything to write home about: bills, two rejection slips, *Newsweek,* and a nasty letter from a book club. People like me shouldn't belong to these "negative option" outfits. I never get the card returned by the deadline, so they send me books I don't want, so I send them back, so they get ticked off and send me snippy "reminders" of how the racket operates. Pointless notices, I should say. I *understand* how they operate; it's *they* who don't understand how *I* operate.

Three people had hung up on the answering machine. Or one person had hung up three times. Or one once and one twice, and what the hell difference did it make anyhow.

I reset the machine, slapped together a peanut-butter-and-mashed-banana sandwich, and downed it and a glass of flat Coke while looking over the news of the week.

That kind of high living can go on only so long, of course. Eventually I toddled back to my bedroom/office, where I stood looking at the desk, the typewriter as if they had only just materialized.

I liberated the aborted Longo report from the typewriter and slipped it into the topmost of the three plastic baskets on my desk. The baskets are optimistically labeled In, Out, and Pending; in fact I distribute items based on which basket looks emptiest at the moment.

Funny thing: The disparate pieces of The Next Book were waiting for me right where I had left them, partly sprawled across the desk, partly stacked on the floor next to it, mostly floating in the vacuum between my ears. Literary gnomes had not sneaked in and completed the manuscript while I was distracted by other things. Little bastards.

I picked up a pencil and poked the blunt end at the most recent pages, as if leery of touching them. In all, there were probably two hundred, two hundred fifty sheets of paper lying around. That's not as impressive as it may sound. Many of those sheets held only a few lines, once the cross-outs were deleted. Some of them were inserts, brief passages intended to fit between existing passages that I was too lazy to retype. Some were just rough outlines, notes to my-self, thumbnail character sketches. Assembled, clean-typed with proper margins and no strike-overs, they probably would come to no more than a hundred and fifty pages. Less than half a novel.

Of course, length isn't everything. In fact, it isn't anything.

Story is everything. You start at the beginning and you go till the end, and whatever length you end up with is the proper length. The problem was, I *wasn't* going. I wasn't writing down dead ends, which is frustrating but not really a waste of time, since even your mistakes and false starts teach you a thing or two. I wasn't writing simply to get words on paper, which frequently can trigger a true creative flow. I wasn't doing anything. It wasn't that the story wasn't there, it wasn't that the words wouldn't come. The story *was* there, and I had been in the business long enough to know that if the story was there the words *would* come if I prodded and teased and cajoled them. I just hadn't been. For a whole bunch of reasons that very neatly jelled together into one. Fear of failure.

When The Book was accepted for publication, I thought the event had shoved me past that little gremlin. I thought it would be clear sailing through The Next Book, and all the Subsequent Books I knew would come.

I was wrong. If anything, success, such as it was, only heightened my fear of failure.

Because, with the first book, I had had nothing to lose; now, suddenly, I did. A tender, green, undeveloped reputation, very fragile, very delicate. I didn't want it bruised.

Now the pages, the sentences, the words that had come together so well *before* I had proven myself—the words that had fairly leaped from fingers to keys to paper, that had flashed through my brain so rapidly and so clearly that I barely had time to get them down—now those words stared at me lifelessly, mockingly.

I dropped the pencil and picked up and skimmed the last few pages I had done. It was like reading someone else's work.

This was the crossroads, I realized. I had three choices. Forge ahead with The Next Book—close my eyes, hold my nose, and dive in. Or dump it and start over from square one. Or dump it and not start over from square one, come to grips with the fact that very, very few people derive any kind of living from the written word, and get on with some kind of adult pursuit.

That didn't sound like much fun.

I rescued the page I had thrown away last night, gathered up the disordered sheets from the desk, and threw them facedown onto the stack on the floor. Then I grabbed my barely legible handwritten notes, a fresh legal pad, a new Bic Roller, lifted the ungodly mess from the floor into the crook of my left arm, and headed for the living room.

Where I dropped my burden in the middle of the ugly rust-colored shag carpet, got down on the floor, and got down to work.

The machine collected two more hanger-uppers: I resolutely ignored them. The third call, however, was accompanied by a message:

"Goddammit, Nebraska, don't you *live* there any more?"

I reached up and grabbed the phone from the coffee table and asked Kim Banner if she thought that was any way to talk to people.

"I wasn't talking to a people, I was talking to a damn machine. I've been trying to get you all day."

"It is for people like you that I spent my hard-earned dough on the aforesaid damn machine. Just leave your dulcet tones on the painfully low-quality tape and I will—"

"Jesus, who wound you up?" Banner's usually hoarse voice had a tight, keyed-up edge to it . . . which I chose to ignore.

"I am suffused with the joy of simple, honest, and productive labor. I've spent the last hour or two rethinking and reoutlining a good portion of the new book—deciding what should stay and what must go and what use to make of the former. My home looks like the wreck of the *Edmund Fitzgerald*, junk everywhere, but me, I'm feeling pretty damn virtuous."

"Allow me to spoil your good mood, then."

"You're welcome to try, although I doubt wheth—"

"Your pal Marlon Abel. He turned up sort of dead this afternoon."

Neither of us spoke for the space of several heartbeats. Then I said, "I was wrong. About your spoiling my good mood, I mean."

There was no good reason to insist on seeing the place. There wasn't even a bad reason. I just wanted to, is all.

Abel's place looked about as I would have guessed. His room was on the third floor, rear. A long, cramped space. A sprung sofa shoved against one bare wall. A card table and folding chairs against the other. A portable TV on a dresser near the sofa, the set turned so that someone lying on the sofa could view it. A twin bed, unmade, shoved into an alcove separated from the main room by a bead curtain and a good imagination.

Sink, mini fridge, and a two-burner gas range filled a nook next to the "bedroom." The bathroom was down the hall.

Abel—or the earthly remains thereof—was long gone, of course. That's why there was no reason for my wanting to see the place. Banner had told me, and I had believed her, but it wasn't enough. Eventually she relented and agreed to meet me and let me in.

"He collected it over there," Banner said needlessly. "Needlessly" because the rusty brown splash across the wall and sofa back said the same thing. "Sometime between eleven A.M. and one-thirty, when the landlady found him. She'd come to collect. No answer at the door, but she heard the TV. She figured he was home, ignoring her, trying to dodge the rent. So she used her key."

"Bet that's the last time she does that," I said. "But if the door was—"

"Spring lock," said Banner. She stepped back a couple

of feet and showed me the inside doorknob. "Push the button, pull the door closed after you, and it's locked."

I made a circuit of the place. It didn't take long. The apartment was a mess—unmade bed, dirty clothes on the floor, a week's worth of dishes in the sink, garbage that wanted desperately to be taken out—but so tiny and so sparsely furnished that it was impossible to spend any time on it.

"Abel must have been standing about where you are," Banner said. "The killer, about where I am. Abel was facing him." I turned away from the bloody sofa and looked at her. "They argued, who knows, and the killer went for his gun." She reached around behind her as if taking a wallet out of her back pocket and came around with two fingers of her right hand extended. "It was fast: Abel didn't have time to duck or try to run or anything. No place to run to: He was cut off from the door, trapped in the room." She cradled her right hand in her left. "*Pow*, one shot. He takes it over the left eye and sits down hard."

I nodded. "Anything?"

"No one heard. The neighbors work days, except for an old man in the basement front, and he's deaf as a post. Just one shot, from a .22, the street's pretty noisy . . . anyone who might've heard it probably didn't, and anyone who did probably isn't saying. It's that kind of a neighborhood. Chances are he'd've sat here a good long time if today wasn't rent day."

"What about his job?"

"He quit showing up a couple of days ago. We checked."

"What about his pal. Patavena."

"What indeed." Banner pulled one of the metal chairs away from the cheap card table and sat. I grabbed the other chair and did likewise. "We dropped by his street-repair job. He didn't show up for work today. We dropped by his residence—makes this place look like the Ritz—but he wasn't there either."

"He clear out?"

"Could be. Hard to tell with these crappy little slums.
This place, for instance. My first thought was, The joint's
been tossed. But it hadn't."

"You're sure of that?"

"Uh-huh. The place is a wreck, but it's too neat a wreck,
if you know what I mean. Too *natural* a wreck. Likewise
Patavena's dive. There's nothing there, but is it because
he took everything and split, or because he doesn't *have*
anything?" She shrugged. "Yours is as good as mine."

"Is there anything to tie Patavena into this?"

Banner ran a hand through her hair. The room was hot
and close, and small dark commas of hair clung to her forehead and neck. She was wearing a pink cotton shirt, light
gray pants, and a gray loose-knotted ribbon tie a little like
the kind James Garner wore on *Maverick*.

"Nothing. There's nothing to tie *anyone* to it. But Abel
and Patavena were as thick as— Well, hell, you know all
about that. It's funny that the one is among the missing
and the other is among the dead."

"Funny."

"Look, Sherlock, what's going on?" Banner's tone was
casual, almost offhand.

"You flatter me," I said. "You think this has to do with
me?"

"Do I think you're involved? No, of course not. Do I
think it involves you? Maybe. You had a couple of run-ins
with these two, Patavena and Abel. I find it peculiar that
one of them suddenly winds up dead."

"But I can't see how or where it would fit into the Longo
investigation."

"Unless they found the money. Patavena killed Abel and
rabbitted. Or someone else killed Abel and scared off Patavena."

"But Longo didn't have the money."

"We don't *know* that."

I sighed. "I don't *know* that the world is round, but all the evidence points that way. Longo didn't have the money. Period. But as for these two characters finding it if he *had* . . . well, I don't think either of them could find his own ass with both hands and a mirror. Guys like them, they live on the fringe, Banner. You know it as well as I do. Look around. The room, the building, the neighborhood. Maybe a junkie killed him for pocket money. Maybe he got into an argument with a drinking buddy, and the buddy didn't feel like losing. Who knows? It's a violent world."

"Uh-huh." Banner wiped the back of her neck. "You're right. And life's full of its little coincidences."

"It is that. A guy and a gal know a guy who used to work where a gal works . . . coincidence."

Banner stood. "That's it: You've had too much of this heat and so have I. Can we go now? Have you seen what you came for?"

I followed her to the door. "I guess so," I said. "Seeing as I don't know what that might have been."

The hallway was no less uncomfortable than the apartment, but a faint draft provided the illusion of ventilation. Banner locked and resealed the apartment, replacing the yellow tape that had been thumbtacked across the doorway. We trooped down filthy bare wooden steps to the alley behind the building, where Banner's unmarked Ford was parked behind my car.

"The old bucket looks pretty good," Banner said with a nod toward the Impala. "Last time I saw it, it was bashed up and splattered with black paint."

"Insurance is a wonderful thing. But looks aren't everything. I'm afraid the old red beast is getting ready to head for that big used-car lot in the sky. And that will be a sad day because (a) I've had this car a long time and (b) there's no earthly way I can afford another one. Unless I find Gregg Longo's hidden millions."

She looked at me. "You said you don't think this has

anything to do with the Longo business. But you don't believe it, do you?"

I looked at the car as if I was thinking of buying it. "No,"
I said. "I don't. Take everything I said—"

"Please."

"—and it *could* be that way. Sheer coincidence. They
really do happen, coincidences—all the time. That's what
makes detective work such a bitch."

"Challenge. My captain says the job's a challenge. He
also says there are no problems, only 'opportunities.' "

"Oh, one of *those* assholes." I sat on the trunk of the
car, my feet on the back bumper. Banner leaned against
the front of her car, arms folded under her breasts. "Mystery
fans hate coincidences, but they make the game. It could
be coincidental that Abel, who was connected to my Longo
investigation, is now dead. Or that Eloise Slater, who also
is connected to the investigation, is palsy with a fellow who's
palsy with *another* fellow whom I've been shadowing in another matter. Or that the guy everyone's so palsy with used
to work with Longo's widow. Or that Lou Boyer's handing
out fifty-dollar notes that were stolen in the robberies attributed to Longo. Or that, or that, or that. Any of them
could be a genuine grade-A, fourteen-karat coincidence. *All*
of them could be. But it puts a real strain on a guy to go
on trying to believe that, you know?"

"*Woh* yeah," Banner said. "And in the meantime there
are seventy-eight thousand unaccounted-for dollars lying
around somewhere. Well, seventy-seven thousand nine hundred, taking away the fifty Longo had on him and the fifty
Boyer passed. All right, ace detective, what do we do now?"

I slid off the car. "I don't know about you," I said, "but
I think I'm going to see if I can eliminate the middleman."

CHAPTER
SIXTEEN

The only thing you can say about Omaha rush hour is that it *is* only an hour or so, not half the night like in the other, bigger cosmopolitan capitals and jet-set havens. Since I don't work nine to fivish like real people, I forget about what the disc jockeys call "drive time," and am trapped more often than I'd like to admit in one or more of the four or five work or school tangles. Of course, it always happens when I'm in the mood to get from point A to point B with minimum hassle.

Like this evening, for instance.

The snake of cars progressed slowly, when at all. Noxious fumes hung in the air, concentrated, held down by the hot, heavy atmosphere. I got stuck behind a moron who evidently had an LSD flashback behind the wheel and didn't come around until the left-turn arrow had gone from green to yellow to red.

I got a look at his license plate as he turned into the wall of outraged horns from oncoming traffic. The familiar blue plates with white numerals. Iowa. But of course. The driving prowess of Iowans is famous, or infamous—too much corn on the brain or something—and stereotypes such as these aren't conjured out of thin air. Go anywhere throughout the rest of the Midwest, from Indiana across to Colorado, Missouri to Minnesota, and you will encounter virtually unanimous concurrence that "IOWA" is an acronym for "Idiots Out Wandering Around."

When I finally got my left turn made, I took a slight risk and quit Dodge for the longer but occasionally faster route along side streets. Sometimes, when the traffic is heavy, the roads less traveled are a good way to make time. Sometimes they're a good way to get killed, too, because the city doesn't have as many stop signs as it could stand, and you never know when there's going to be another clock-watching fool—from Iowa, likely as not—also trying to make time but traveling in a route perpendicular to yours. That's the "slight risk" I mentioned.

But I lived to tell the story and to pull up across and down from Monroe James's little brick-façade house. I sat behind the wheel, trying to think of a good way of determining whether the house was occupied without tipping my hand. In the crime novels, the hero or sometimes the villain sinks a coin in a pay phone, and if no one answers, concludes that the joint's vacant. Nice dream, but in real life it isn't so easy. Modern telephones are equipped with bell silencers; people unplug their modular phones; people use answering machines to screen their calls. I figured I might as well save my quarter.

I was still considering and dismissing possibilities when a by now familiar-looking Toyota made the turn off of Western Avenue and came to a rest against the curb three houses down from James's.

Interesting, I thought. Although I would have bet cash money that the two men would have another meeting of the minds ere long. Their parting the evening before, in the lot of the Antenna Lounge, had had that see-you-soon look to it.

Desotel climbed out of the Toyota, pulled a gray leather-and-suede attaché out after him, and sauntered down the sidewalk toward the house. The front yard sat four, four and a half feet above street level. Three brick steps took you from the sidewalk to a narrow brick walk that took you to a wider brick stoop at the front door. Desotel mounted the steps, knocked on the door, and waited. He didn't so much as glance at his surroundings.

Monroe James admitted him. He gave a quick one-two glance up and down the street. It was a nervous response is all; he didn't take the time to actually *see* anything. Like me in my car, for instance.

I drummed a muted tattoo on the steering wheel. Waiting. Thinking.

Something was going on in there. Hell, child, you don't have to be a detective to know that. Even if I hadn't been tailing Loverboy for days, even if I hadn't tripped over James two or three times already, even if I wasn't an innately suspicious man—if I had just stepped out of my house across the street to pick up the paper and saw one guy park three doors down when there was plenty of free parking right in front of the house he then proceeded to walk up to without looking left or right, then saw the other guy sneak a peek both ways up the street when he let the *first* guy in . . . well, wouldn't *you* wonder what that was all about?

Me too.

I pulled the little Vivitar tele camera from under the front seat and unwrapped it.

Whatever was happening inside, or was about to happen, was illegal or embarrassing enough for the participants to be behaving *very* oddly. A photographic record of the proceedings might be just the thing to persuade Loverboy to do right by Mike Kennerly's client and end all that alienation-of-affection nonsense.

There was little doubt in my mind that such blatant blackmail would be abhorrent to Kennerly and that he would refuse to be a party to the foul deed. Luckily for him, I wasn't going to tell him the gory details.

I checked the camera, making sure the battery was properly juiced up and the film indicator still showed 2, meaning I didn't have a roll of snapshots of the underside of the front seat as photographed through a Ziploc bag. For important junk like this, I always advance the film to the second exposure. If you've ever noticed that, when you get your pictures back from the drugstore, the first snap is almost always fucked up somehow, you know why I always start out a roll of film with a picture of the palm of my hand.

I slipped the camera into my shirt pocket and scoped out the street. Two kids on bikes, towing a kid on a skateboard. But they were toward the far end of the block and moving away from me. A guy up the street was adjusting a sprinkler on his lawn, but he would go inside soon: He wasn't dressed for yard work. No one else, no one that I could see, at any rate.

I got out of the car. Almost as an afterthought, I slid back in and fished the revolver out of the glove compartment. Then I went around and opened the trunk and rummaged through my Official Double-Oh-Seven Disguise Kit.

The disguise kit is this: a bunch of junk.

Disguise isn't Sherlock Holmes making himself up to look like an antiquarian book dealer; it isn't wigs and false noses and cheeks stuffed with tissue paper—all that Peter Sellers shtick in the Pink Panther movies. Disguise is more like sleight of hand, diverting the audience's attention. Putting on or taking off a jacket. A hat. Glasses, plain or dark. That's disguise.

From the disguise kit, an old blue Nekoosa Paper cardboard box with a lift-off lid, I pulled out a pale blue workshirt and quickly donned it over my sport shirt, tucking the tail into my jeans. I found a dark-blue workman's cap and put it on. A small clipboard with a pale green pad went under my arm. I closed the trunk lid.

Lo: Unspecified Tradesman of the Month.

The James house was the third from the corner. I walked down to the corner, left the sidewalk, and wandered around the side of that house and into the backyard.

Meter reader, I had decided. Gas, electric—didn't matter.

No one pays the least attention to meter readers, as long as the meters in question are in the yard and not the basement; no one knows when they come and go, what they look like, what exactly they do.

I checked the electric meter on the back wall of the house at the end of the block. It looked okay to me, and I pretended to make notes to that effect on the clipboard. I did the same thing at the next house. It seemed to me that those people were pulling a lot of juice: That disk whirligig was doing about ninety R.P.M.

James's house was next. The electric meter was conveniently located near the dining-room window. The air-conditioner compressor was conveniently situated beneath the dining-room window. The dining-room window was inconveniently closed, the air conditioner being at work, but a guy can't have everything.

I didn't glance around before hopping up onto the compressor. Glancing around makes you look suspicious.

I did, however, duck back down almost immediately, which wasn't exactly a nonchalant thing to do. But how was I to know Desotel and James would be sitting at the dining table, not three feet from the window? I couldn't hear voices, not with the racket from the compressor under my feet.

I snatched off the cap, shoved it into my waistband at the small of my back, and had another go at it. Slowly.

The dining room wasn't so much a room as an extension of the living room, which was at the front of the house. The kitchen, presumably, was to the left, my left, behind and above the garage. At the dining table, as I mentioned, their backs not quite to me, were Desotel and Monroe.

On the table in front of them were two briefcases, gaping wide—Desotel's posh gray leather/suede attaché and a cheap vinyl case, the kind you can buy in any dime store.

Both of the briefcases were loaded with cash.

"Loaded" means *loaded*. An ant would not have had room to curl up for a catnap in either of the briefcases.

If this was what a "financial consultant" did for you, I thought, I have *got* to get one.

Monroe James was doing the talking. I could tell by the way his head and hands occasionally moved: No words came through the glass or over the noise of the air conditioner. I had the feeling he was still trying to sell Desotel on something. But what? Clearly not insurance. No drugs, jewels, industrial papers, or illegal arms were lying around. Desotel had carried in only one of the cases, meaning James had already had the other there. Did one contain counterfeit money? Which one, James's or Desotel's?

At about that moment I realized three things: (a) I was in a good spot to be noticed by one or more of James's neighbors, who might easily call the cops; (b) I was in a good spot to be noticed by Desotel or James, if either happened to glance toward the window or even just had good peripheral vision; and (c) if I didn't want to have to tail Loverboy all over hell and half of Arkansas until I was old and white, I had better quit rubbernecking and get busy.

I slid the Vivitar out of my shirt pocket, thumbed the telephoto-lens button, and composed the frame. As it were.

Desotel was the perfect model. He sat as still as the pink flamingo in your front yard, Monroe James to his left, the two briefcases full of cash on the table in front of them. I held my breath and squeezed off a shot . . . wondering if the auto-flash would give me away. It didn't. The camera didn't think it needed the extra light and I didn't need to take off like a scared rabbit. I took half a dozen more shots, making sure to get enough of Desotel's profile to ensure easy identification.

I would have played out the roll, but seven shots were all I could work in before Monroe James noticed me and all hell broke loose. Or most of it, anyway.

James yelled—through the glass, I couldn't hear what,

but I caught the drift. Desotel jumped eighteen or twenty feet off his chair. James leaped up and headed for the front door.

Pausing only to grab something from a china-cabinet drawer in the living room.

I didn't feel like sticking around to see what he had grabbed. But I was in a lousy position for getting back to the car. By going out the front way, James would effectively cut me off from the street. I should have had an escape route planned before I ever climbed up to the window . . . but I didn't. The story of my life. Now I scanned the backyards in a panic. I could cut through them to the next street . . . but the yard behind James's and the next one down were both fenced in by tall redwood-stained barricades that Spenser could probably leap over like a kangaroo, but not me.

And I'd be wide open to a shot if I tried to skirt the yards either way.

I hopped down from the compressor, snatched the cap from my waistband, and wrapped it around my fist before I smashed in the window in the door of James's walk-out basement.

James had a TV/exercise-room arrangement in the main area. Very nice, although I had scant time to admire it as I zigzagged between furniture and workout equipment.

I made it to the stairs as James, having come around the house, made it to the basement door.

The door was at an angle of about forty-five degrees from the stairwell. James had a .45 in his fist. He stopped inside the doorway and fired spasmodically, popping off three or four shots that shattered the drywall several inches wide of my head. I crouched and turned and fired back. It was just like on television, where the bad guy lets go a hundred rounds that all miss while the good guy squeezes off one well-aimed shot that ends the show, only this time the good guy missed, too. James's Exercycle would never be the same, but at the moment he didn't seem to care. He flung himself against the south wall, the wall into which the stairwell was set. I couldn't see to aim unless I stuck my head out from the stairwell, in which case he'd blow it off like a gopher's. He couldn't see to aim unless he crept down and peered around into the stairwell, in which case, I'd return the compliment.

That's the sort of situation that can give you an upset tummy real fast, so I decided to get out of it A.S.A.P.

Two choices: Duck through the connecting door to the garage, which was at my back, and get across the street to my faithful old bucket of bolts. Or duck upstairs and take my chances with Loverboy.

If the object of the lesson had only been to get the goods on Loverboy, I'd have followed the former course, gotten the hell out of there, and taken my pictures to Fotomat. But the game had expanded. There were things to be got to the bottom of.

I hightailed it upstairs.

The door opened into the kitchen. I slammed it shut behind me and grabbed a vinyl-covered chair to prop under the doorknob. A ridiculous precaution: The hollow-core door wouldn't stand up to a strong sneeze, and James could always circle around and come back through the front door if he felt like it.

Desotel was still at the dining table. He had his attaché closed and latched and was struggling with the other one. It was overstuffed and he was too greedy—or stupid, or rattled—to dump some of the cash and split.

I waved the gun at him. "Lousy idea, Jonny."

He pushed the cheap briefcase away from himself like it was on fire. It slid off the table and hit the floor, bundles of long green spilling on the carpet.

"Don't shoot me!" he squealed.

"Okay. Sit down."

He did. I hurried through the living room to the front

door, which stood open. I slammed it shut and gave the dead-bolt knob a twist.

"Talk fast, Loverboy, the clock's running. What's going down?"

Desotel was white. Not white as in Caucasian, white as in Casper the Friendly Ghost.

"Did you kill Monroe?" The way he shivered, you'd have thought the room was cold. It wasn't.

"I haven't killed anyone today," I told him. "Yet. Talk."

"I— We're switching the money."

Switching the— "You're laundering James's dirty cash."
He nodded frantically.

"Through the club. The restaurant."
More nodding.

That was what James had been trying to sell Desotel— the idea of running dirty money through the bar and restaurant that Desotel managed. And a tony, overpriced place like the Olympic Club . . . hell, when dinner for two sets you back a hundred bucks, *thousands*, much of it cash, had to go through a joint like that every day. The bar probably did even better. Laundering the loot would be easy and, if you were halfway careful, safe. You pay suppliers with dirty money, you make change with dirty money, you slip a little into the daily deposit, only a little, so no one gets suspicious . . . fantastic. You could probably change over ten thousand inside of a week before anyone asked a single question. With a suitable percentage going to your inside man, of course.

The briefcases held the first exchange. Desotel's—that is, the club's—nice clean green for James's filthy lucre.

James's . . .

"Where'd *he* get the dough?"

Desotel jumped—not because of my stern, authoritarian voice but because James hit the basement door, hard.

"Where?"

"Some woman. I don't know—I *swear*—"

James was really putting his shoulder to the door now. It was a contest: Would the door splinter before the chair legs slid far enough on the linoleum for the chair to topple?

Time to be scampering along. I didn't want any bloodshed, especially as there was a chance the blood might be mine. I turned from the kitchen to Desotel.

"Fun time's over, Jonny, you know that, don't you?" He nodded stupidly. "There isn't going to be any game." I pointed at his briefcase with the gun. "That goes back to the club safe or on to the bank or wherever it's supposed to be." He nodded.

"Now," I barked.

He jumped up, grabbed the case in both hands, clutched it to his bosom like it was a babe, and ran for the front door.

There was a shot, muffled and flat sounding. Wood exploded and littered the kitchen.

I took off behind Desotel.

Another shot, then a crash and a clatter that must have been the chair flying.

We hit the bricks and split off—Desotel south, me north. I fancied hearing the basement door shatter as we came out of the house, but it may have been my overactive imagination.

Or not: I heard an animal wail behind me as I yanked open the door to my car. I risked a look back. Monroe James stood on his front stoop, the .45 in his right hand, the other hand clenched in impotent rage. Desotel was midway between the house and his car—he'd had farther to run. James raised his gun. A perfect shot. If he was even just a passably decent marksman, he could plant one between Desotel's shoulder blades, no sweat.

And then what? This was middle-class America, not Marlon Abel's neighborhood. There would be no conveniently deaf neighbors. There would be cops and reports and witnesses . . .

I had turned, cradling my gun hand in my left, sighting James. Waiting. Sweating.

Had James fired three shots at me in the basement, or four?

Four plus two on the basement door added up to an empty gun.

Three plus two added up to one bullet left for Jonathon Desotel's back.

Sweat ran down my face and into my eyes. My heart tried to break out of my chest. I couldn't stand there and watch James murder a man. But if James's gun was empty . . . Who was the murderer then?

Waiting. Sweating.

Until defeat washed over Monroe James, and he lowered his right arm and let the big, ugly gun drop into the shrubbery alongside the stoop.

CHAPTER
SEVENTEEN

The sky was yellow and had the look of rough, faded fabric. The atmosphere was as it had been all day: airless: heavy, damp, and hot. The kids who played in the yards and the streets didn't notice, didn't care, but their parents did. They sat on lawn chairs in the shade or toyed lazily with gardening tools or, more commonly, were nowhere to be seen, holed up in their air-conditioned palaces with beer and TV, no doubt.

I drove quickly from Monroe James's neighborhood. The wave of defeat that had so obviously washed over him might easily be replaced by the strong current of revenge. I didn't want a confrontation: My quarrel was not with him. So I opted for the better part of valor—running—and made tracks. I had cut down to Happy Hollow Boulevard, taking it not northward, toward chez Nebraska, but southwest, across Dodge and into Elmwood Park, behind the UNO complex. The park was verdant, lush, cool and almost dark. Kids on bikes and young moms and dads behind strollers slowed my progress, but I didn't care. I tooled along the curving, seemingly aimless drives, one eye on skateboarders and the other on the rearview mirror.

No gray Celebrity Eurosport intruded on the idyllic scene. Eventually the park spit me out onto Pacific Street. I managed a left turn against the fag end of rush-hour traffic, heading east.

A breeze had come up, not a cool breeze, exactly, but one that carried, instead of the sticky, oppressive mugginess, the clean smell of rain. I drove slowly along residential streets and enjoyed the breeze. Or pretended to, at least, while my head swam in a dark pool of random thoughts and feelings. The stream of consciousness you've heard so much about.

The car went to Carolyn's house. I was only a passenger.

The sky had darkened. The windows in the house were even darker. I went up onto the big enclosed porch and tried the bell. Deep in the house, a harsh buzzer sounded. There was no other sound. There was no answer, even after several more buzzes.

I went around the north side of the house. At the rear, ancient, bowed wooden steps led up to a tiny back porch. I hiked up them and pounded on the door that opened to the kitchen. Nothing. The curtain on the door gapped a little: I peered through and saw the gloomy, gray room. Empty.

Next to the back door was a double-hung window, open perhaps an inch from the bottom. You can guess the procedure: I used a ballpoint pen to punch a hole in the screen, widened the hole to accommodate my arm, got the screen off, raised the window, and climbed in. Inelegantly, but in.

"Carolyn . . . ?"

The empty room repeated it back to me.

I wandered through the kitchen, into the dining room, into the living room, into the entry. Nothing untoward, nothing out of place except for the usual clutter of everyday life. The house was closed up, and stuffy. The kitchen window appeared to be the only one left open. An oversight.

The stairs were wide, dark planks with a runner of pale

carpet down the center. I went up, not caring about the creaks and squeals the steps made underfoot.

The bedroom doors were closed, and the top-floor landing, cut off from even the gray light from outdoors, was nearly pitch-black. I brailled across it to the door of Carolyn's room.

"Carolyn?"

The doorknob was made of some heavy, dark metal. It was cool in my palm. I turned it, and the door swung open easily and silently.

The room was empty.

I hit the wall switch—the old two-button kind—and yellow light burst to life in a bowl overhead. The room was neat and orderly, much as I had seen it the other night, except for the absence of Carolyn, half-naked and half-asleep on the bed.

I sat on the mattress and the springs beneath it groaned, as they had groaned beneath Carolyn and me the night before. The night before, when twenty years caught up with us, or with me at least, and the story left unfinished all these years finally got an ending. Of sorts. Do such stories ever really end?

Images exploded in my brain, dark scenes captured in the brief, deceptive illumination of a flashbulb. Scenes at once repulsive and exciting, shameful and sensual. Scenes that should shame you but instead set you to grinning like a fiend. Carolyn, her hands tied loosely at the small of her back. Me, frozen in that half moment when power and passion rise in equal proportions and the voice in the back of the brain says, *Yes! Take her!* before the other, saner voice cuts in and says, *This is not a power game, this is about sharing, not owning,* and prevails. But the first voice, while still, is not gone, is never gone.

I lay back on the bed and contemplated the ceiling fixture.

There was nothing that said Carolyn couldn't simply be out for the evening . . . working late . . . shopping. Hell, on a date even. Nothing at all.

I stood and crossed the room and swung open the closet.

Hard to say, having never seen the inside of the lady's closet, but there seemed to be an awful lot of bare wire hangers staring back at me. There seemed to be some gaping gaps amongst the shoes neatly lined up along the floor, too.

I tried drawers in the dressers and nightstands. Again, the inventory was low. One dresser drawer was empty.

Bathroom cabinet. Empty except for a tin of Band-Aids.

Garage (also locked, but what are mere locks to the likes of me?): Empty except for lawn mower, shovel, other garagey junk.

"Ah, Carolyn," I said to the dank, vacant space.

Only the cobwebs heard.

CHAPTER
EIGHTEEN

By the time I got down to Ralston, the sky was a sheet of yellow blotting paper onto which someone had tipped a bottle of india-ink wash. The breeze had grown up and become a wind, which wound the medical arts building's U.S. flag around its metal pole and whipped the chain-link runner against it so rapidly and regularly that it sounded like a bell ringing. The wind dried the sweat on my back and arms as I stepped out of the car, and I shivered.

I felt old, tired, used up. My muscles ached, the residual effect of my encounter with Abel and Patavena the day before, compounded by my more recent exertions at Monroe James's house. Now my head was beginning to think that maybe it would start aching too, just to stay in step. I wanted to go away, I wanted to be somewhere else, I wanted to be some*one* else.

A few tentative drops of rain kamikazied into the windshield. I closed the car door but only just, making about as much noise as you make buttoning a shirt. I scanned the trailer park but saw nothing and no one unusual. Nothing and no one at all.

Overhead, leaves of tall old maples sighed and whispered

roughly as they shook themselves like great green animals. I trudged across the pea-stone drive to the little metal house. Another darkened house—but this one ominously so, not sadly, as Carolyn's had been.

Correction: The house was *almost* dark. I noticed watery yellow light making its way through a translucent shade over one tiny window as I took one giant step up onto the wooden platform at the front door.

The skinny aluminum door was closed but not locked. I turned the hooklike handle and pushed with the side of my fist.

The living room was black. Drapes and shades were pulled, and what little graying light sneaked in around and under them had all the illuminating power of a safety match. I paused to let my eyes adjust. Hulking shapes appeared in the darkness. Furniture, righted and set back against the walls, where it must have stood before Abel and Patavena had had at it the other day.

The house shuddered in the wind and I, involuntarily, mimicked it.

I picked through the dark and unfamiliar territory like a blind man. My outstretched right hand touched hard, cool, round-edged plastic. The kitchen counter. Flat wall to the left. Cold metal to the right: the refrigerator. Ahead of me, a long yellow rectangle—a ribbon of light bleeding through a one-inch gap in the bedroom door. I moved toward the light, a moth to the flame. The door swung to soundlessly.

The yellow light emanated from a fat white candle on a bedside table. Its flame burned high, flickeringly, throwing weird nightmarish light against the walls of the small room.

Eloise Slater lay on the bed, facedown. She lay still, but her body seemed to undulate in the wavering candlelight. Blood drummed dully in my ears. I crossed the room and put two fingers behind the angle of her jaw.

I didn't feel a pulse. I didn't have time to, because I jerked my hand away, startled, when she jumped and made muffled noises as I touched her.

The noises were muffled because Eloise's mouth was filled with a red ball-gag whose black straps were fastened securely behind her head. She was naked but for a thick-looking black blindfold that covered her eyes and ears and was fastened behind her head with two small silver padlocks. She was bound to the bedposts with the leather-and-nickel manacles that I had seen before. Her wrists were crossed over her head and secured with leather ribbons, left wrist to right bedpost, right wrist to left. Her legs were separated by a long black bar contraption fastened to her ankles.

Eloise's body glistened in the candlelight. Glistened with perspiration, glistened with blood—tiny beads of blood that stood up in the sharp, vicious-looking welts that crisscrossed her shoulders, her buttocks, her thighs. A short-handled whip lay on the bed between her legs.

Something white and plasticky dotted her backside and was collected in the cleft and the small of her back. Eloise flinched and moaned into her gag as I touched the stuff. Congealed candle grease.

"She who hesitates is lost," I quoted quietly as I moved to undo the gag. The red plastic ball was too big for her mouth. Getting it out took some work, and it's fair to say it hurt her more than it did me, although small mewing sounds were the only protestation she made, or could. "Looks to me like you hesitated too long."

To the garish, flickering shadows I added, "Wouldn't you agree, Carolyn?"

And Carolyn Longo stepped from the darkened bathroom doorway into the tiny circle of light emitted by the candle.

"How did you know?" she said calmly.

I dropped the saliva-dampened gag and stood. Eloise Slater was silent but for swallowing, jaw-stretching noises.

"Know what? That Eloise had the money, or that you would try and take it away from her?"

An odd, enigmatic smile traced its way across Carolyn's otherwise expressionless face. "You choose."

"I knew Eloise had the money because she was here. Now. If she hadn't been, it'd still be a toss-up in my mind between her and you."

"I had the feeling you were suspicious of me."

"I suspect everybody, as they say in the movies. I knew you'd try to take it away from her because here you are . . . unless there's some other reason for your being here . . ."

Carolyn said nothing.

"Uh-huh. As for knowing you were still here . . . well, that was a lucky guess. The moment demanded something dramatic, and I felt obliged to oblige. If you hadn't been here, I'd have felt foolish."

"Yes, but why me? Why not somebody else?"

"I admit that Al Patavena looked like a real contender for a while there—until I saw Eloise lying here. Not Patavena's style at all, this kind of theater. He's more the aluminum-baseball-bat type, as I know from experience. You made yourself suspect by coming on so strong about how the cops were riding your ass and so on—probably so I'd feel sorry for you, take the case, and lead you to the girlfriend you were pretty sure your husband had had."

She looked almost embarrassed. "I knew you didn't do much detective work anymore. And I wasn't sure how you felt about me."

"Good thinking, but it didn't hold up. Bill Jurgenson kept telling me the feds *weren't* leaning on you—why would he lie? Ma and Pa Kent were parked on the porch across the street—the house *you* said the cops were staked out in. Finally, you tripped yourself up. You indicated to me that the feds had searched your house several times, but when you were yelling at Jurgenson last night you said they had gone through it *once* already."

No reply.

"None of this really jumped out and hit me in the head. It all just contributed to a vague feeling of unease I'd had

all along—unease about you and why you *really* wanted me
to investigate Gregg. Tonight, when I was weighing things,
sorting them out, these little inconsistencies and doubts kept
floating to the surface. When I came across a load of dirty
money tonight that was in the process of being laundered
for a woman client, I felt that the field of contestants had
suddenly narrowed. By the way, did you manage to ice
both Patavena and Abel on your lunch break today, or just
Abel?"

Her head jerked in surprise. " 'Ice'? You mean kill? I
never killed anyone."

"Then that leaves the Bitch Goddess." I looked down
at Eloise and raised my voice slightly so as to be heard
through the blindfold that covered her ears. "What's the
story, Queenie? The boys come back and hot-box you until
you got tired of it?"

Eloise remained still. But I knew she had heard. I knew
that there must have been three names on her list of people
who could cause her grief. Abel. Patavena. And Nebraska.
Abel had been dealt with. Maybe Patavena, too: It remained
to be seen whether he would turn up and, if so, whether
he'd be breathing when he did. As for Nebraska . . . well,
it didn't take a great deal of imagination to picture what
would have become of our hero if he had accepted Eloise
Slater's taunting invitation.

I turned to Carolyn. "Abel and Patavena were unimagina-
tive souls. Having taken it into their fat heads that Eloise
had the money—I'm sort of to blame for that, I'm afraid—
they weren't about to give up the idea. Eloise knew there
was only one sure way to shake them. And she knew enough
to do it in such a way and such a place that she couldn't
be connected to it."

"You're good at what you do," Carolyn said softly.

"This? Oh, this is the easy part now. Connect the dots.
It goes like this: Eloise had the money and, being crafty,
was keeping it socked away, laying low, keeping her life

exactly as it had always been. Because she couldn't be absolutely certain that no one knew of her existence. She couldn't be positive that the cops—or someone—weren't keeping an eye on her, giving her rope."

I looked again at Eloise.

"Stop me if I get off track, will you?"

She might have been asleep for all the response she gave.

"*I* queered that deal. When I came on the scene, Eloise must have realized that it was only a matter of time before real live Establishment-type cops came swooping down on her. It was time to scoot along. But the loot was dirty. To exchange some of it for nice clean cash, she enlisted your pal—and hers—Monroe James."

Carolyn nodded, as if confirming something in her own mind. "All those questions about him . . ."

"Now you know. You and James working in the same firm, that was coincidence. The bane of us pure-hearted private eyes' existence. Existences. Whichever. I wouldn't be at all surprised if Eloise was one of the jurors in that Reilly trial that caused our Monroe so much trouble. In any event, James was the man Eloise thought could help her with her little problem. She was right. James latched on to the manager of a *very* upscale bar-and-restaurant here in this Paradise on the Plains, and if all had gone according to the diagram, Eloise would have had, I don't know, five or ten thousand pristine bucks on her person right now. Plenty to get out of town on, *way* out of town."

Carolyn's smile was hideous in the lurid light. "I *thought* she looked like she was expecting someone else when she answered the door."

"It's always nice to have these loose threads tied up, isn't it—oops, no offense, Eloise. What I'm interested in is, how'd you find out about her?" I indicated the helpless woman. "I never told you her name."

"Yes, you did. You and Jurgenson, talking in my basement. You must have been near the furnace. Your voices carried right up the ducts. And you had mentioned that she lived in Ralston. There aren't too many Eloise Slaters in Ralston . . ." Her shrug was negligible. "Getting the address was as easy as opening the phone book."

"Getting her to tell you the location of the seventy-eight grand—or what of it that Monroe James doesn't have—must not have been." I waved a hand at the scene on the bed. "What finally did the trick, the whip or the hot wax?"

"Neither." Carolyn brought her right hand up and out of the shadows. "*This* did." In her fist was a gun, a gun that looked very much like the .22 I had taken away from Marlon Abel the other day. I had no reason to think it was not the gun that had done in its ex-owner.

"Just like in the detective books," I said. My voice sounded a little high-pitched, even to myself. I cleared my throat and said, "I've really got to start keeping better track of things like that. You never know when they're going to come back to haunt you." I drifted, very slowly, toward the foot of the bed, my right hand outstretched, palm up. "This is just a little too melodramatic, Carolyn. Why don't you hand over the iron and we'll end this thing now before someone gets hurt—really hurt."

"I thought you liked drama." She raised the gun ever so slightly but ever so definitely in my direction. I stopped my negligible advance toward her. "You should love this," she said. "It's just like one of your detective stories, isn't it?"

Yes, except I don't care that much if Spenser or Scudder or whoever gets drilled.

I said, "Where'd you get that popgun?"

She looked at it as if just noticing it. "I found it in the closet when I was looking for the things to tie her up with." She glanced toward the closet. The thought of rushing her flashed across my brain and disappeared just as fast. I couldn't have gotten around the bed in time to reach her before she pulled the trigger. I followed her glance at the sliding doors near the foot of the bed. One side of the closet was open, and junk spilled out of it and onto the carpet. Dark shapes, mostly, in the dim and flickering light. Clothes. Shoes. Items that may have been more of Eloise's playthings. More clothes . . .

"I hit her over the head," Carolyn was saying. "God, I thought I had killed her, the way she just . . . dropped. She was still conscious. I was going to just look for the money while she was out, but . . ." Carolyn looked at me. Her eyes were black in the dim light. "I brought her in here. You had talked about the . . . equipment she used with Gregg. I found it." She looked at Eloise, an alabaster mannequin in the bizarre light. "It was just as well. I'd've never found the money on my own."

"Under the front steps."

Carolyn's eyes came back to me, wide. "You knew?"

"I guessed. I'm guessing all over the place. The landscaping work out there looked recent—and ongoing. Easy to wrap the dough in plastic, scoop a shallow dugout, bury the loot, cover it with a layer of dirt, a landscape cloth, a layer of stone. Easy to get to. You could do it in broad daylight if the neighbors weren't too nosy. Incidentally, you might not want to get your fingerprints all over that thing." I nodded at the gun. "I have the feeling it's the gun that killed Abel, probably Patavena, too."

The smile had left her face. "Don't worry. I'll get rid of it." She looked long at me, her face impassive. When she spoke, her lips barely moved, her words barely made it across the room to me. "God, Ivan, I wish you hadn't come here."

"I'm beginning to feel the same way. By the way, you were wrong."

"Wrong?

"I don't like this at all."

A smile made its way across her face, most of it collecting in one corner of her mouth. It was a small, sad smile, a

smile of regret, a smile of resignation. Or, hell, maybe it
was just a trick of the light.

"I mean it," Carolyn said. "I mean it. I really wish you
had stayed away."

For Eloise's benefit I said, "What she's getting at is, she
was just going to leave you here like this and vanish into
the night. Someone would find you, and she wouldn't have
to worry about your tattling on her. It'd be embarrassing
for you, but what the hell." I glanced at Carolyn. Her cheeks
were wet. Moisture inched into the lines between her nostrils
and the corners of her mouth, but her face was as expressionless as a china doll's.

"Now, unfortunately, she has to kill you. What's worse,
she has to kill *me*, too."

Across the bed from me, Carolyn sniffed wetly. "I didn't
mean to hurt anyone. I was just going to take the money
and go away. I wouldn't even *be* here except I came back
after I loaded the money in my car to take the gag out of
her mouth so she could breathe okay."

"A humanitarian with a gun. What a refreshingly quirky
combination."

The wall that held in her emotions cracked, crumbled,
and fell away. "Goddammit," she sobbed harshly. "I only
wanted the money. I deserve it. My husband *died* for it.
It's *mine*." She looked at me almost pleadingly, willing me
to believe her, agree with her, give my blessing to the deed—
robbery, murder . . . *my* murder.

I said, "Gregg didn't die for it."

The half-hysterical sobs stopped abruptly. She looked at
me through streaming eyes, snuffled loudly, wiped her nose
with the back of her left hand.

"He died *because* of the money, but not *for* it. The sick
irony is, it was the biggest money trouble Gregg was ever
in . . . and he wasn't in it. The only stolen money he
ever saw was a crummy hundred bucks that *she* gave him"—

I jerked a thumb at Eloise—"and which he never even got to spend. He gave half of it to Lou Boyer and died with the other half in his jeans. He didn't even know it was stolen."

Carolyn looked from me to Eloise and back—stupidly, as if drugged, as if just coming out of a deep and unrestful sleep. "But . . . But then . . ."

"She did." I repeated the thumb gesture. "You know why Gregg came here, Carolyn: to have Eloise do to him what you've done to Eloise. Picture Gregg in that position: trussed up, helpless. He can't see, he can't even hear too well. Eloise would leave him like that for . . . who knows? A good long time. Long enough to take Gregg's car—a precaution—and go make some money. Dressed in men's clothes, covered from head to foot, she could pass for a slightly built man. And *did*." I moved quickly—and recklessly, but Carolyn was temporarily too confused to react—and scooped up a handful of clothing from the floor. "See? Here are the work gloves." I dropped them on the bed, near Eloise's left leg. "Long-sleeved shirt. Men's. Small." I dropped it. "And this." I held up the dark ski mask for a moment before letting it fall to the bed.

Carolyn made no attempt to mask her surprise and confusion.

"That's why Gregg didn't pay his gambling debts," I said, "why he didn't skip town, why no one could tie him to the robberies. He never had the money."

"Why didn't *she* leave town?" Her eyes were on the naked woman.

"What for? Everyone had been looking for a holdup *man*, as she had planned all along, and when Gregg died with stolen money on him, everyone thought they *had* their man." Carolyn's moist eyes had come back to my face. "Gregg died for nothing," I said quietly.

She sniffed. "It's still my money."

"Possession is nine points of the law," I agreed. I was

near the foot of the bed, where I had stayed after grabbing the stuff off the floor. Now I began to edge around the foot, very, very slowly. I made my voice go low, slow and soothing, the way you might talk to a frightened animal. "Look, Carolyn, you haven't done anything really stupid yet. Don't start. Give me the gun, give me the money, and you can walk away. I'll turn it over to the cops and feed them some kind of line. I'll keep you out of it, I'll keep Eloise out of it, too, to guarantee she won't squawk. She couldn't nail you without nailing herself. Everybody's in the clear." That was an out-and-out lie, of course: Eloise Slater had murdered one, maybe two men, and it would take someone with colder blood than mine to simply ignore that. But I didn't share that thought with Carolyn.

"Everybody's in the clear," Carolyn echoed. "And poor. Do you know what it's like, Ivan? To not know if there's going to be enough to cover the bills? To have people calling the house, collection agents, creditors, wanting their money now, *and you haven't got it?* To be scared all the time—scared you'll lose everything, they'll take everything away?" The waterworks had started again. "Do you *know?*"

"Oh, vaguely," I answered. The gun had remained in her fist, forgotten. Not by me: by her. We were separated by the width of the double bed and another two or three feet, the distance between Carolyn and her side of the bed. If the bed had been narrower, or Carolyn had been standing closer to it, or I was in better shape or any kind of shape at all, I might have contemplated doing something stupid like the guys on the TV crime shows. Instead I took a couple more baby steps and rounded the foot of the bed.

My thinking about the gun seemed to remind Carolyn of it. She raised it slightly, aiming at my breastbone.

"I don't want to do this, Ivan." Her voice shook. Tears dripped from her chin onto her shirt.

"Then don't. Quit it now. You know you can't get away with it."

Despite herself she laughed at the Saturday-matinee dialogue. I felt my mouth twist into an involuntary grin. "Sorry, but the Private Detective Code requires me to say 'You won't get away with it,' or words to that effect, at about this point. The truth is, your original plan—leave the Priestess of the Whip as is and just vanish—probably would have worked. This one certainly won't. Eloise wouldn't have reported you to the cops; how could she? But kill us and there *will* be an investigation. Your name *will* come up. And you *will* be conspicuous by your absence. You'd be surprised how fast seventy-eight grand, or however much is left, evaporates when you're on the lam, honey."

Her dark eyes scanned the room as if looking for a way out. Suddenly they seemed to catch fire, and she looked back at me excitedly. "Then . . . Then I won't run. I'll go home and stay there, and I'll hide the money, and I'll tell the police I don't know anything about— No! I'll tell them you came to my office today, because you did, there are witnesses, and you told me that you had set up a meeting with someone who could tell you more about Gregg and the money. And that's *all* I'll say. They'll assume something went wrong, someone double-crossed you, whatever. Because there's nothing to connect me with her or this place." Her eyes locked on mine. "That will work!"

The hairs on my neck came to attention, mainly because she was right.

"Well," I said, fighting to keep my voice level, "that's better than saying you're going to make it look like I killed Eloise and then killed myself, which is what Hollywood would have you do. What if I tell you that I brought the police with me and they now have the place surrounded, which is what Hollywood would have *me* do? . . . No, I didn't think so."

She had raised her right arm. Now she extended it toward me, bringing up her left hand to support her wrist. Her hands trembled. Her shoulders shook.

For a small gun, the .22 looked awfully big.

"I'm sorry, Ivan." She sniffled. Her cheeks shone with moisture that danced and glittered under the flickering candle flame. "There's no other way. I don't want to hurt you. I don't even want to hurt *her*. But there's no other way."

"Carolyn . . . Carolyn, this is a big mistake . . ."

"Good-bye, darling . . ."

CHAPTER
NINETEEN

The moment comes in every detective story. Things look bleak for the intrepid hero. He has brilliantly pieced the mystery together, but in such a fat-headed fashion as to leave himself high and dry. The villain has the advantage. But our noble knight-errant, while seeming to prattle on aimlessly, has subtly maneuvered himself into a position from whence he can conveniently douse the lights. The room goes black. A shot explodes into the darkness. A struggle ensues. Someone bites someone else on the hand. The gun skitters across the floor like a spooked cat. Another struggle ensues. Protagonist and antagonist lock in mortal combat, the gun at the center of the struggle. Again it spits fire. There is an awful moment of suspense . . .

It didn't go quite so elegantly in this case.

In fact, it didn't go elegantly at all.

Carolyn's finger tightened on the trigger of the .22.

The barrel of the gun erupted in a white-hot flashbulb explosion.

I dived for the floor on my side of the bed and hugged it like it was my long-lost mother.

And someone held a red-hot rod to my left biceps.

I shouldn't have been standing there when Carolyn's gun went off. Another nanosecond and I wouldn't have been, I'd have been on the floor, hiding behind the bed like any sensible person. But there it was, and there I was, and there the bullet was. Irresistible force meets not-quite-immovable object.

Funny. In the movies it happens in slow motion. In real life, when it happens, it happens fast, impossibly fast, an unintelligible blur of events, of sounds, even of smells. You don't put the components together until later. If you live.

I lived. The problem with the first-person narrative is that you know, or ought to, that the bullet didn't kill me. Of course, in the moment I wished it had. I couldn't decide whether to throw up, crap in my pants, or break down and cry, so I did none of the above. Swallowing hard to keep what was in my stomach in my stomach, I flipped onto my back and reached over my head to grab a leg of the bedside table. I tipped the table and the candle extinguished itself harmlessly. Better late than never. I took a splash of wax across my face, like a razor slash, but it was nothing compared to the fire in my arm.

My face was wet with sweat and tears. I reached over with my right hand, tentatively, fearfully. The slug had caught me in the upper left arm—I'd begun to move, otherwise it would probably have taken out my Adam's apple—spun me around and knocked me on my butt. They always do that, bullets. Except on television.

I took my hand away and rubbed the hot, sticky fluid between my fingertips. Blood. My blood. What I get for trying sweet reason when what I should have done was grab the .38 out of my back pocket and blow Carolyn's pretty little head clean off.

Still not too late for that: I rolled halfway onto my left side and yanked out my gun with my right hand. The effort probably hurt monstrously. It was hard to tell, because already the pain in my arm was starting to feel remote, as if it was someone else's injury, not mine. My arm was beginning to feel sort of numb. So were my lips and my fingers. I was beginning to feel kind of dopey, too—more than usual—and I caught a kind of nervous giggle, a *tee-hee-I'm-not-dead* chortle trying to sneak out on the end of a fast, ragged breath.

I swallowed a few more times and concentrated, concentrated on listening for Carolyn, concentrated on staying conscious, concentrated on staying alive.

I think I may have drifted off, but only for a matter of seconds. Then I registered the sound someone's harsh breathing—mine?—and the night wind grabbing the house and shaking it angrily, and a faint swishing sound like a brush on canvas.

Carolyn, feeling her way across the blackened room, her fingers grazing wall, furniture.

I waited, trying to hold on to the bare whispers over the sound of the wind and of my heart pounding.

An eternity later I kicked out, kicked again—kicked something that yielded.

Carolyn. She cried out and fell on top of me and was all arms and legs in the darkness, thrashing, fighting, clawing.

Inevitably my injured arm ended up on the receiving end of one of her blows, and an Independence Day display went off behind my eyes as pain rocketed from my arm to my brain. I struck out just as blindly as she had, caught her hard—I don't know where, but hard—and felt her weight suddenly lifted from me as she crashed against the wall opposite the bed. It knocked the wind out of her, and I heard her half-sobbing, half-hiccuping breath as she tried to get it back.

"Carolyn . . ." I croaked.

I got up onto my right elbow and tried to drag myself toward where she must have fallen. The side of my hand, the hand that held the gun, touched bare flesh. A leg, an arm, whatever it was, it jerked away from me, accompanied by a kind of scared-animal cry.

"Carolyn—"

There was a sound in the darkness, a sound I didn't recognize, and then the impact of something flat and hard on the side of my head.

The room got very bright.

And then it got very dark.

I didn't lose consciousness. I heard Carolyn drag herself up, crying, heard her stumble out of the room and to the front door. I heard that door open and close. I heard a fitful rain hammering the roof, like handfuls of gravel that someone occasionally tossed up. I heard an engine sputter to life. But for all the use I was, I might as well have been fettered like Eloise.

I don't know how long it was before I could cajole my arms and legs into going back to work. It didn't matter. Two minutes would be more than enough time for Carolyn to have headed off in any of four directions. With seventy-eight thousand dollars, less however much Eloise Slater had given to her friend Monroe James.

I groped for and found a light switch and, after I got my eyeballs put back in, started untying Eloise.

CHAPTER
TWENTY

The Douglas County sheriff's department found Carolyn that very night, or, more accurately, early the next morning. She was in her car. The car was a burned-out husk that had lighted the night sky above a lonely, rain-slick highway west of town. There had been no accident. The car was neatly pulled off to the side of the road; there were no skid marks, there was no sign of trouble. There was only a charred, melted, grotesque wreck. The sheriff suspected foul play and investigated accordingly. Nothing came of it.

If there had been any money in the car, it was long gone. One way or another.

There was no reason, no official reason, to suspect that Irish Tim Callinan had had anything to do with the incident. Certainly that kind of strong-arm stuff would have been out of character for him. But Gregg Longo had owed Tim a great deal of money, and Carolyn had to have had more than fifty thousand when she left the Slater place. I always sort of wondered, What if the cars that I thought had been following me *had* been? What if Irish Tim had had me tailed since the night I drank Jameson's with him in his personal citadel? What if his minions had let me lead them to Eloise, to Carolyn, to the money . . .

I also always sort of wondered why Carolyn hadn't finished me and Eloise Slater when there was nothing either of us could have done about it. If Irish Tim—or someone else— had had her number, then she still wouldn't have gotten away with the loot. But she wouldn't know that at the time. As far as she knew—as far as I still know for sure—only Eloise and I could have caused trouble for her. Still she let us live.

I wonder about that. But I think it was a good decision.